A CURE FOR SUICIDE

A
CURE
FOR
SUICIDE

JESSE BALL

PANTHEON BOOKS, NEW YORK

F
BAL

This is a work of fiction. Names, characters, places,
and incidents either are the product of the author's imagination
or are used fictitiously. Any resemblance to actual persons,
living or dead, events, or locales is entirely coincidental.

Copyright © 2015 by Jesse Ball

ING
3/16
24 —

Library of Congress Cataloging-in-Publication Data
Ball, Jesse, [date]
A cure for suicide : a novel / Jesse Ball.
pages ; cm
ISBN 978-1-101-87012-9 (hardcover : acid-free paper).
ISBN 978-1-101-87013-6 (eBook).
1. Man–woman relationships—Fiction. I. Title
PS3602.A596C865 2015   813'.6—dc23   2014206919

www.pantheonbooks.com

Jacket image: Cyanotypes by Karen Fuchs
Jacket design by Kelly Blair
Book design by Maggie Hinders

Printed in the United States of America

First Edition
2 4 6 8 9 7 5 3 1

In honor of TB,

and for GGG

1

[
THE
PROCESS
OF
VILLAGES
]

THE EXAMINER closed the gate behind her with a swift, careful motion. She listened to it shut, and then proceeded. Ahead on the right, outbuildings loomed in the murk of early morning. The sun's rise was slow; she felt it behind her, coloring the barn with the least possible gesture.

On she continued up the path. A rut in the ground showed a gurney had been dragged past in the night. These were the signs she knew well—it was her profession, her task to know them. A hollow anticipation stiffened in her and grew to a faint point of tension in her cheeks. The gentlest village. Here she was in the gentlest village. The path led her past the barn and on to a tall Victorian house, the door of which stood open. In she went.

The rooms were furnished simply and with taste. Everything about it was identical to all the other houses she had ever been in, in all the villages she had ever been in. But this, this was the gentlest village. There would be things that were different.

In the sitting room, there was no one. In the parlor, no one. Up the stairs, she went. In the first bedroom, no one. In the upstairs sitting room, a piano—and no one. In the second bedroom, which she entered softly, as softly as could be, there was someone. Indeed there was.

There was a man lying flat on his back, breathing shallowly, and staring with his eyes open at the ceiling. His chest moved up— and down—and up. His hands trembled slightly.

She stood there watching, noting every detail of his countenance.

He did not notice her.

SO, THIS WAS THE CLAIMANT. This, then, was her task. She looked at him awhile and when she was satisfied with this first look, she went to the study and took out a piece of blank paper. She placed it on the writing desk.

From her pocket she drew out the letter she had received the day before. She unfolded it.

+ +

Report to Gentlest Village D4. The stamp on this letter will gain you admittance.

Claimant is on schedule three, as per size and responsiveness to medication, which will have been administered 12 hours prior to your arrival. This gives you 20 and one half days before Mark 1.

You were selected based upon your recent success. It is expected that you will serve with even greater distinction going forward.

In First House protocol for Gentlest Village, you will write daily reports, which will be collected from the locked desk in which you leave them. The unlocking and locking of the desk will signal the desire for a pickup to be made.

There need be no verbal contract with the claimant, as in your previous work. Prior to Mark 1, the claimant will be utterly biddable, indeed nigh helpless.

The manner of treatment is your choice. First House examiners need not follow treatment routines such as you have been accountable to in the past. Reprocessing decisions need not be confirmed. Move of station to Gentler Village will be made based upon your written recommendation, and can be effected within an hour of your writing.

> All success in your endeavor,
> General Secretary
> Emmanuel W. S. Groebden
> Process of Villages

+ +

On the blank paper, she wrote:

+ +

Have arrived, seen claimant.

+ +

She put both letters in the desk and closed it.

1

—THIS IS A CHAIR, said the examiner. A person is made
in such a way that he can sit where he likes. He can sit on the
ground,

she knelt and patted the floor

or even on the table itself,

she patted the table.

—However, if you are in company, it is best to sit in a chair
unless there is a good reason to sit elsewhere. In a chair, one
can sit with good posture, that is, with the skeleton set into good
order.

He looked at her with puzzlement.

—The skeleton, she said, is a hard substance, hard like wood,
like the wood of this chair. It is all through the inside of your
body, and mine. It keeps us stiff, and allows our muscles
something to pull and push on. That is how we move. Muscles
are the way the body obeys the mind.

—Here, she said. Come sit in the chair.

She gestured

The claimant came across the room slowly. He moved to sit
in the chair, and then sat in it. He felt very good sitting in the
chair. Immediately he understood why the house was full of
chairs.

—They put chairs wherever someone might sit.

—They do, she said. And if your needs change, you can move
chairs from place to place. Come, let us eat. We shall walk to the
kitchen, and there we will get the things we shall eat; also, we
will get the things on which we shall eat, and the things with
which we shall eat. We will not eat our food there; we'll go to

the dining room, or to the enclosed porch. This will be a nice thing for us. Having gotten the food and the implements, we will decide whether we want to eat on the porch or in the dining room. Do you know how we will decide that?

The claimant shook his head.

—You do. Think carefully. Say what comes to mind.

—If it is a nice day, outside . . .

—That is one reason, one of many reasons, why a person would choose to sit outside. It is a good reason. It is always best to have a good reason for doing things, a reason that can be explained to others if you must. One should not live in fear of explaining oneself—but a rational person is capable of explaining, and even sometimes likes to do so.

—Rational?

—A person whose life is lived on the basis of understanding rather than ignorance.

—Am I ignorant?

—Ignorance is not about the amount of knowledge. It is about the mechanism of choosing actions. If one chooses actions based upon that which is known to be true—and tries hard to make that domain grow, the domain of knowledge, then he will be rational. Meanwhile, someone else who has much more knowledge might make decisions without paying any attention to truth. That person is ignorant.

—A mechanism, she continued, is the way a thing is gone about.

They went into the kitchen. On the wall was a painting of a woman feeding chickens with millet. The millet poured from her hand in a gentle arc. Around about her feet the chickens waited in a ring, looking up at her. When the arc made its way to the ground, they would eat.

Beside it was a photograph of a hill. There was a hole somewhere in it.

The claimant paused at these wall hangings, and stood looking. The examiner came and stood by him.

—What is different about these? she asked him.

He thought for a while.

—About them?

—What's the difference between them? I should say. When I say, what is different about these, I am making two groups— them and the rest of the world. When I say between them, I am setting them against each other. Do you see?

—This one happens less often. He pointed to the woman with the chickens.

—Less often?

—If you go looking for them, outside the house, he said, you could probably find the other one, no matter when you looked. But, you can't find this one.

—Why not? Because it is a painting?

—A painting?

—Because it is made by hand—with strokes of a brush? Or for another reason?

—I didn't mean that, he said. I am tired. Can I sit down?

—Yes, let's go to our lunch. We can return to this later.

THE CLAIMANT sat watching her. He was in something she called a window seat. She had her hands folded and was sitting in a chair. They were in a room with what she called a piano. It made loud noise and also soft noise.

The examiner was a girl. The claimant didn't know that word, but it is how he saw her. He had known others, he was sure of it. Her soft yellow hair fell about her shoulders, and her bones were thin and delicate. He felt that he could see where the bones were through the skin. His own bones were larger.

She was helping him. He didn't know why. It occurred to him that he hadn't asked.

—Why am I here? he said suddenly.

The examiner looked up from her book. She smiled.

—I was waiting for you to ask that. Actually,

—she looked at a little clock that lay across her leg,

it is just about the right time for you to be asking that. Nearly to the minute.

She laughed—a small, distinct laugh.

—You are here because you have been very sick. You almost died. But, you realized that you were sick, and you went to get help. You asked for help, and you were brought here. It is my job to make you better. You and I shall become good friends as you grow stronger, and as you learn. There is much for you to learn.

—But, he asked, where was I before?

—In a place like this, she said. Or in some place so different as to be unknowable to us when we are here. I can't say.

—Why do I keep falling asleep?

—You are learning—learning a great deal. It is too much for you, so your body bows out. Then you wake up and you can continue. It will be like this for a time. I have seen it before.

—Are you the only one like me? he asked.

—No, no, no.

She laughed to herself.

—There is a whole world full of people like us. Soon, you will meet others, when you are ready.

—How will we know?

—I will know, she said.

ON THE THIRD DAY, she pointed out to him a gardener. The man was in the distance, trimming a bush.

—There, she said. There is one.

He stood and watched the man for at least an hour. The man had gone away, and the claimant stood looking at the bush that had been clipped, and at the place where the man had been. He asked the examiner if the gardener was likely to be in that spot again. Not that exact spot, she said, but another near to it. This was the gardener window, then, he said. I can watch the gardener from here. They are all gardener windows, she said. There are others, and others. It's a matter of how far you can look, and if things are in the way. She took him to another window. Out of that one, he could see three people in a field, in the extreme distance. They were scarcely more than dots, but they were moving. At this distance, she said, you can't tell if they are men or women. They could even be children, he said. It might be hard to see a child that far off, she said. They could be, he insisted. The examiner did not tell him: there are no children in the gentlest village.

On the fifth day, she told him about fire, and explained what cooking was. He found fire to be very exciting. He could hardly bear the excitement of it. She wrote this down.

On the sixth day, he closed a cupboard door on his hand, and cried. She explained crying to him. He said that it felt very good. In his opinion, it was almost the same as laughing. She said that many people believe it is the same. She said there was perhaps something to that view, although of course, it appeared to be a bit reductive.

SHE WROTE THINGS in her notes, things like: Claimant is
perhaps twenty-nine years of age, in good health. Straight black
hair, grayish brown eyes, average height, scars on left side from
<childhood?> accident, scar under left eye, appears to be a quick
learner, inquisitive. Memory is returning relatively quickly.
Claimant is matching given data with remembered data—a
troubling development.

ON THE MORNING of the seventh day, he refused to get up. She told him to get up. He refused.

—What's wrong?

—The other day, you said that I almost died. That I was sick and that I almost died.

—You were sick. Now you are convalescing. You are regaining your strength. You are young and have a long life ahead of you in a world full of bright amusements and deep satisfactions, but you have been sick, and you must regain your ability to walk far and parse difficult things.

—What did you mean when you said I almost died?

—It isn't very much. It is a small thing. The world is full of organisms. You are an organism. A tree is an organism. These organisms, they have life, and they are living. They consume things, and grow, or they have no life, and they become the world in which other organisms live and grow. You almost became part of the world in which organisms live, rather than that which lives. It is nothing to be afraid of—just . . .

—But it would be the end? he said. There wouldn't be any more?

—It would be an end, she said. Do you remember the conversation we had, the second night? About going to sleep?

He nodded.

—What happened?

—I went to sleep, and then in the morning everything was still here.

—Death is like that. Only, you work in the world with a different purpose. The world works upon you.

—How did I die?

—You didn't die. You nearly did.

—How?

—We will talk about this later, when you have more to compare it with. Here, get out of bed. Perhaps it is time for us to go for a walk. Perhaps we should leave the house.

He got up and she helped him dress. They had clothes for him, just his size in a wardrobe that stood against the wall. They were simple, sturdy clothes: trousers, shirt, jacket, hat. She wore a light jacket also, and a scarf to cover her head. He had never seen her do this. I often cover my head, she said, when I go outside. One doesn't need to, but I like to.

They went into the front hallway, an area that he had not understood very well. It appeared to have no real use. But now when the door was opened he could see very well why there should be this thing: front hallway. He went out the door and down the stairs and stood by her in the street. He could feel the length of his arms and legs, the rise of his neck.

Going outside, he thought—it is so nice! The things that he had seen through the window were much closer. He could see houses opposite, and suddenly, there were people inside of them, and lights on. There was no one in the street, though. He walked with the examiner, arm in arm, and they went up the street a ways.

The houses looked very much the same. He said so.

—Do you know, she asked—do you know which one is ours?

He looked back in fright. The houses were all the same. They were exactly the same. He had no idea which one was theirs. She saw his fright and squeezed his arm. I will take you back to it, don't worry. I know which one is ours.

The street wound past more houses, and they gave way to buildings that she called shops. No one was in these shops, but the windows were full of things that she said might be bought. He did not understand, and did not ask.

On down they went to a little lake. Fine buildings were in a circle around the lake. There was a bridge in the lake to a little island (as she called it), and on the island there was a small house with no walls. They sat in it, and she poured him a glass of water from a pitcher that sat on a tray on a bench at the very center.

WHEN HE WOKE UP, he was back at the house again, in bed. It was the afternoon, he guessed—as light was all in the sky.

—Did I fall asleep again?

But she was not in the room. He went out to the landing. There was a carpet, but the old wooden boards of the house creaked beneath his feet. He winced, trying to step as quietly as possible. The railing ran along the top of the landing. The balusters were worked with lions and other beasts. He knelt by the edge and listened.

She was speaking to someone else. He couldn't hear what she was saying. The door shut, and she came up the stairs. When she saw him kneeling there, she smiled.

—Did you wake already?

—Who was that?

—Friends. They helped to bring you here. You didn't think I could carry you all by myself?

—Can I see them?

—Not yet, she said.

—What about the other people—the people in the other houses?

—Not yet, she said.

—How will you know?

—I will know.

SHE WROTE in her report,

++

As I stated before, in the case of this claimant, the dream burden of his treatment was severe. His every sleep period is marred with nightmares. He is still in the first period, prior to Mark 1, so he remembers little to nothing of this, but it is a cause for concern. If it continues this way, I may need to directly address it. He talks in his sleep, muttering about a person who has died, and speaking with a vocabulary that he does not possess during the day. It is my hope that reprocessing is not necessary. He is mid to high functioning and could do very well as things stand but would lose much after a second injection.

++

She leaned back in her chair and her gaze ran along the wall. There was a stopped clock, an embroidered handkerchief in a glass case, and an antique map. The map showed the known world as of a time when nothing was known. How apt for the Process of Villages.

She wrote:

++

The previous case that I worked on involved a woman prone to violence and anger. None of that struggle is evident with this current claimant. It appears that his difficulty may have been entirely situational. If that is so, there is a good chance that our process will bring him to balance, as there may be no flaw whatsoever in his psyche.

++

—GARDENER IS THERE! He's there!

She came to the window where the claimant was sitting.

—Is it the same one—or a different one?

—This one is wearing . . .

—Glasses.

—The other didn't have them.

—Is that a good way to tell them apart? she asked.

—It is one way.

—What if I were to wear glasses?

She took a pair out of a drawer and put them on.

—Would I be a different person?

She did look like a different person with glasses on, but he didn't want to say that, so he said nothing.

—It is usually safe to assume that a person is different if their physical characteristics are different, said the examiner. But even then sometimes people change—by accident or on purpose—and the same person can look different. Likewise, two people can look very alike.

—Or be exactly the same, he said.

—What do you mean?

—Twins are alike. They are the same.

—But even if the bodies are the same, the minds inside are different—their experiences are different. They are different people.

—Even if they can't be told apart?

—Even then.

—I knew someone, I think, who was a twin.

She looked at him very seriously and said nothing.

—She had a twin, but the twin died.

—How do you know this? asked the examiner.

—I remember it.

—But not from life, she said. You remember it from a dream. When you sleep at night, your mind wreathes images and scenes, sounds, speech, tactile constellations—anything that is sensory—into dreams. One feels that one has lived these things, of course one does. But dreams are imagined. They are a work of the imagination.

—What is the imagination for?

—It is a tool for navigating life's random presentation of phenomena. It enables us to guess.

—But I am sure that I knew her.

—Know her you did, but it was in a dream. You may dream of her again. That is the world where you can meet such a person. The actual world is different. For you, it is this house, and the street beyond. It is the lake at the center of the village, and the gazebo in the lake. It is the meal we take together at midday, and again at nightfall.

She sat for a moment quietly.

—Do you remember the book that I was reading to you from?

—About the poacher and his dog?

—Yes. You remember how real it seemed? Well, it is not real. It just seems to be real. And that is just a toy of words on a page— not anything close to the vibrant power of the mind's complete summoning that you find in the night. Is it any wonder that you believe it to be real? That you confuse memory and sleep's figment?

He shook his head.

She took off the glasses, and put them in the drawer.

—I still feel that you are different with glasses, he said.

She laughed.

—People do look quite different with glasses, I suppose. I suppose that must be true.

—Will you play for me on the piano? he asked.

She went to the piano and opened it.

—I can know that it is you because you play for me on the piano, he said. Someone else wouldn't do that.

—So, she said—you believe an individual's function and service are identical to their person?

She began to play.

He looked out the window again. It was open, and the air was moving now and then, sometimes in, sometimes out. Or, it must move out whenever it moves in. It couldn't just move in, or it would all end up inside. But, he supposed, that wasn't entirely impossible. After all, he was completely inside.

He put his arm out the window and felt the air on it.

Below, the neatly trimmed yard lay flat on its side. The street unrolled from left to right, and beyond the houses, other streets could be seen by the white chalk of their surface. The tops of houses could be seen downhill, the glint of light off the lake in the distance. In the long fields of the distance, and in the canopies of the trees, in waves at their edges, he felt a coy energy. It was as though the edges of things were where the greater part might be hidden—where he could find more.

But he need not go even so far as beyond the room to find more—for just then, the sound of the examiner's playing was moving him. He sat still in the window, but he could feel himself moving. It was a peculiar sensation, to have things called up out of one's depths. A person can travel when they hear music, just as much as by walking.

He said it to himself and it sounded good.

—A person can travel when they hear music, just as much as by walking.

The examiner looked up. She stopped playing.

—Some can. It is a matter of inner faculty.

—I don't know . . .

—Can you feel what you think I am feeling when I play? Can you watch me and imagine how I am feeling? There are people who can. Some people go beyond that, and imagine that they can feel what inanimate objects feel, or what animals feel, or even attribute feelings to a landscape, or a distant house. When you go on a journey of empathy such as that, it rouses sensations that have long sat deep within. Thus you feel as you do now. It is even possible, she continued, to empathize with a person you hope to be, or a person you have been, long ago in a city or a town you may never see again.

—A city?

—We live in a village. It is a place . . .

—A place of houses.

—That's right. A city is like that, but larger. The houses are stacked upon each other, so that they rise up into the sky like mountains, only much steeper. The air is full of them—houses wherever you look. In some places you can't see the sky at all unless you look straight up. Millions of people—a hundred times a hundred times a hundred—wander the streets in things called crowds, large groups of people who need have no common purpose.

The claimant laughed.

—You can't expect me to believe such a lie. You think you can just tell me anything!

—Oh, I assure you it is true. Never fall into the mistake of believing, said the examiner, that things are everywhere the way they are here, wherever here is, wherever everywhere is.

—THERE IS A THING I want to tell you about, she said. It is called naming. Many things have names. You know that. The bottom post on the staircase is called the newel post. The staircase is called a staircase. The post is called a post. The bottom of the staircase is called the bottom. These are all names. People can have names, too, and naming is a privilege. In human history, names have been used as a form of power. Poor families, for instance, would sometimes have three or four sons, and those sons would simply be given numbers for names. First son, second son, third son. Some people would be named just for their position. Blacksmith, or Miller. In fact, that naming system was so strong that there remain people today who have as part of their names those old positions.

She paused.

—Can you think of someone you speak about in that way?

—The men who work outdoors.

—You call them gardener. And if you spoke to them that way, they would understand. This is why it is useful—because it is effective communication. You speak to them, and they understand. Now, let us imagine that such a person had a different name—a name that had nothing to do with what he or she did. What would you say to that?

—It wouldn't make sense, he said. How would you get such a name? There would be no reason for you to have it instead of a different name.

—That's true. What would you call me?

—I would call you, examiner.

—That's right, and why am I an examiner?

—Because your work is to examine people and things and help to achieve balance.

—That's what I told you, and I have shown it to be true through my actions. So, to you, a sound name for me is examiner. However, that is not my name. That is the name of my position. In the world, there are many examiners, but there is only one person with my particular allotment of cells who stands in my geographical and temporal position. That person is myself, and so I have a name to help differentiate me from other people who are similar to me.

—But, if you are the only one in your circumstance, why do you need a different name? Shouldn't your circumstance alone be the name itself? If it is specific to you?

The examiner laughed.

—Very good, very good. But it isn't necessarily so, because not everyone has perfect information. So, if they saw me on one day at the lake, and then a week later, by that distant field, they might not know that I was the same person, unless I had told them my name. If I had, they could speak to me and use my name, and thereby confirm that it was me.

—But what if there were two of you with the same name?

—That is a problem. It is—and it comes up. In any case, I have a name. That gardener has a name. Everyone has a name. Everyone but you.

—Why don't I have a name?

—You don't have a name because you are starting over. You are beginning from the beginning. You are allowed to make mistakes and to fail. You don't need to do that under a real name, a name that will stay with you. We give you the freedom to make every conceivable mistake and have them all be forgotten. So, for now you will have a conditional name. You will have a name while you are here in this first village. Here your name is Anders.

—Anders. Anders.

He said it quietly to himself.

—Can you say it again?

—Anders, she said.

—Anders. Anders. What shall I call you?

—You can call me Teresa. That is not my real name either. It is the name for the examiner that orbits you. Teresa and Anders. Names always function this way, though people don't think about it. They only exist in reference to each other.

—I'm not any more Anders to that gardener than I was a moment ago.

—You aren't. And his name is hidden from you. Perhaps forever.

—Where did my name come from? What does Anders mean?

She thought for a minute.

—I believe it is a Scandinavian name, or perhaps it is German. Let me say completely how it was for me in the moment I named you Anders. That is as close to the meaning of this use of Anders as we can get.

She stood up and went to the window.

—When I was young, there was a girl who lived on the same street as me. Her name was Matilda Colone. She was very pretty and she wore beautiful clothes. She was the envy of everyone at my school, and she was blind. How can that be? Of course, it isn't silly for grown people with circumspection and wisdom to envy a blind person who happens to be extraordinary. However, for children to do so—when the world is so bright and good to look at . . . you may imagine that it is surprising.

He nodded.

—She was elegant and calm. She learned her lessons perfectly. She had a seat in the classroom by a window, and the breeze would ruffle her hair or the scarf she wore, and we would all look at her and look at her and look at her. Matilda Colone, we would say under our breath. The teachers adored her, and everyone wanted to be her friend. But, she needed no friends, and would have none. Of all the things she had, and she had many, the best thing was that she had a brother, named Anders, and he sat beside her in class. He walked beside her to school. He brought her her lunch. He held her coat; he held it up, and then she would put it on. He was very smart, smarter than anyone in the class, except perhaps Matilda, but it was hard to say, because they would never cross each other. It was a school for the smartest children in the region. We all loved her so much that we could almost weep.

—What happened to her?

—This was in the old days. Her father shot himself, and she and Anders were separated and put into homes. Some years after that she died of pneumonia.

—Anders, he said to himself.

—Yes, she said. Its meaning is: a brilliant and trustworthy companion who exceeds all expectation.

—But you did not name yourself Matilda.

The examiner smiled. She did a half turn and her dress swirled lightly. To the door she went, and looking back, she said,

—That is a matter of taste. My respect for Matilda and Anders is such that I am not trying to supplant them. I am just invoking them. The tragedy of Matilda's life is too great for us to speak of it without seriousness. Would I use her name for a purpose? Perhaps I might. Would I name a child Matilda? Certainly. But, it is a name ill suited to a costume. As I plan to retire this name, just as you will retire Anders, it is better to choose a less severe name.

The claimant looked after her in the doorway where she stood. The wooden door frame was worked with pastoral scenes— harvests and crop-sowing and landscapes covered in snow. Beneath it and between it, she seemed almost to kneel, although she stood.

—Teresa, he said. I want to know more about your life.

—It is a part of the help I bring you, she said. One day, you will have heard so much that you tire of it!

EACH NIGHT, the examiner would say to the claimant
something like this (not this, but something like it):

Tomorrow we are going to wake up early. I am going to wake
early and you are going to wake early. This will happen because
I am sure to do so, and I will come and see to it that you are
woken up. Then, I shall dress and you shall dress, and we will
go downstairs to the kitchen. In the kitchen, we shall have
our breakfast and we will enjoy the morning light. We will
talk about the furnishings in the room. We will talk about the
paintings and the photographs that we talk about each morning.
You will have things to say about them and I will listen. I will
have things to say to you about the things you have said. In this
way, we shall speak. After breakfast, we will wash the dishes
we have used and we will put them away. We will stand for a
moment in the kitchen, which we will have cleaned, and we will
feel a small rise of pleasure at having set things right. It is an
enduring satisfaction for our species to make little systems and
tend to them.

Yes, she would continue, we shall go on a walk to the lake, and
perhaps this time we will walk around it to the small wood
at the back. There we will find the trees that we like. Do you
remember them? Do you remember that I like the thin birch
that stands by the stream, and that you prefer the huge maple
with the roots that block the path? Do you remember when you
first saw it, and you ran to it? We shall go there tomorrow, and
spend as much time as we want to sitting with those trees, in
that quiet place. And when we have done that, we shall come
home, walking fast or slow, and we shall . . .

And in this way she would go through the day and give him a
sense that there was something to look forward to, and nothing
to fear.

ON THE ELEVENTH DAY, the examiner brought a sheet of paper to the dining room table. She asked the claimant to sit opposite her. In her hand, she had also a thick object made of paper.

—This, she said, is a book. It is one of our ways of codifying and keeping human knowledge. When it cannot be kept in a person's head, this is one method of keeping it safe. It is a good way of moving ideas from one head to another, as it only requires one person's time to do it, and not two.

She opened the book and showed him the letters. She wrote them out on the paper.

—I think, he said. I think I can do it.

—Can you, she said.

He took the pen and wrote on the paper:

A room and a table and a pen. I am writing this.

He wrote it perfectly. The examiner took a deep breath.

—Very good, she said. That means that I will not need to teach you how to write. What a good thing. Our use of writing will be the following: I want you to take some time in the morning to write down the dreams that you can remember from the night before.

His face became downcast.

—I know that you have dreams, she said. I have watched you toss and turn. You even cry out now and then. Let us attend to them, and perhaps we can settle your sleep.

—I will try.

—It is difficult for a person to write down dreams when anyone is nearby, so I am going to go out on the porch and read

for a little while. You can come and join me when you are
done.

She placed a notebook on the table.

—You can write your dreams into this. It is nicer than the loose
sheets.

—Do you have any questions about writing?

—How is it that I can remember to write—but you had to show
me how to button a shirt?

—Time is passing, she said. You are coming back into yourself.
Perhaps other good things, other helpful things will appear.

—Is writing the same as thinking? he asked. Maybe that's why
I didn't forget it.

—It is not the same, although it can almost be. We shall see
what your writing is like. I am eager to know. Some trace the
origin of writing to the origins of granaries, thousands of years
ago. Before that, man wandered as a hunter, but once he began
to till the land, there was more food than could be eaten in a day.
What was there to do but put it in a building and save it? Then,
one suddenly feels the need to write down how much grain has
been put in the building. And, that's when writing begins—
or so some say. The other thing, she confided, that starts with
granaries, is the keeping of cats. They came to the granaries to
hunt mice and rats, and they have stayed ever since. Cats and
writing, perhaps they share a little of the same nature, then?
That is a joke, she said.

The examiner left the room. Her footsteps crossed the hall,
paused at the door, and sounded on the porch.

ON THE FIFTEENTH DAY, she sat at the writing desk, making her report. The noise of the claimant's breathing could be heard through the open door. A window was before her, and through it she could see clouds and a sky surrounding them, and beyond it, a moon that was hardly a sliver. Maybe there wasn't even a moon there to be seen.

+ +

The claimant's memories intrude at an alarming rate. The cause is clearly his dream recollection. I have chosen a course of reintegration, to begin tomorrow. He has completely regained his written language, and writes with great composure.

A sample of his dream records:

—— ——

I see the face of a woman as she lies in a bed. I am sometimes near enough that her face is all I can see, as though she were leaning over me. But it is I that am leaning over her. At other times, I feel I am far away and I can see the bed, the room, and her—all of them as small as objects on a table, and as still. I am sure that she is dead.

When I see her, I feel that she is surrounded by images, and although I can see her, I cannot see the images that blur her face. Somehow I feel that they are images of our happiness— that we were happy and knew one another. I feel that these things are hidden from me, and that she has carried them into death and I can never know them again.

And then I am flying through a long tunnel in the darkness and there are stars all about me, and finally I realize that I am just water—I am just the surface of a pond. I ripple and when I ripple, I sail through darkness until the ripples settle and I can see again. And when I see, what I see is the sky above and it is full of pinpricks of light.

When I woke up this morning, I had just been sitting in a
station where there were huge machines to carry people. I
was waiting for someone, and I was holding a paper bag full
of presents. I wore a long coat—it was cold—and a hat and
gloves. A child was crying or blowing its nose on the bench
beside me. I felt someone was coming to meet me. And always
someone comes up from behind and calls to me, a man. I
see him, but I don't recognize him, and he goes away, not
as in life, but back the way he came, backward, fluttering
backward, and all the trains leave the station the same
way, and even the child is gone, there's just a bench and a
handkerchief, and I am the one crying.

—— ——

Troubling, to say the least.

The course of his recovery is peculiar. We are already on
difficult ground. He has begun to insist that he remembers
this woman, and he asks me incessantly to explain details of
his dreams—which would lend him a larger view onto the life
he led. All the same, I favor transparency, where it is possible.
Perhaps it is not possible here.

+ +

THE EXAMINER sat the claimant down at the dining room table one afternoon.

—Do you remember, she said, how I told you last week that there was a thing called writing, how I explained it to you, and showed you about it, how we practiced thinking about it, and imagining doing it, and how it could be used to record dreams?

The claimant looked at her with a bit of confusion.

—You remember how I told you several of my dreams? How I wrote them down and showed them to you? And I told you, if you wanted to, you could try to dream them yourself? And you have been trying, all this last week?

She set on the table several sheets of paper—in her handwriting, the dreams she had written out for him.

—I suppose, said the claimant, I suppose I do. It is hard to remember. I feel like I have been dreaming.

—You have been dreaming, said the examiner, you have been, and, Anders, you have been dreaming the dreams that I told you to! You have been so very successful. Now it is time, for the very first time, for you to write yourself.

She brought out a pencil and a leather notebook and set them before him.

—Please write down in this the dreams I have been sharing with you—the ones you managed to also have. And write down any you have that branch off of those—those are important, too.

The claimant held the pen and looked down at the notebook. He looked up at her and down again.

—Do you need some help? she asked.

—I just, he said, I am having trouble remembering about . . .

—About . . .

—About what is what.

—Well, the first dream we worked on for you, the first of my
dreams that you were to have—and this was only because you
were having such trouble remembering your dreams at all—the
first dream was of a thing called a train station.

—A train station?

—A place with large machinery that runs on wheels. Large
boats with wheels that travel along metal rails. They carry
people in and out.

—I remember, he said. I remember it.

—You see, she said, you were successful—you had the dream
when we decided you should.

—I was sitting on a bench, he said. I was waiting for someone.

—The dream, she said, is one that I often had as a child. You
see, I was in boarding school some of the time, and so I would
wait for my parents at the large station. It felt like it was always
winter, and I was always in a coat, I was always sneezing. I had a
cold, I believe.

—Yes, he said, in the dream, I also had a cold!

—Sometimes it was me, and sometimes it was a child who sat
next to me.

—Do you remember the other dreams that we worked on?

—No, said the claimant. I can't seem to remember.

—There was one, a dark and difficult dream. It is of my mother.
I told you about her. She died of a fever when I was seventeen.
She was still very young then. That dream is just a single image,

just her in a bed, lying with her eyes closed. But all around her there flutters the life of my family, and the world that we lost when she died. Don't you remember, said the examiner crossly. Don't you remember at all? This was the first success that we had—on Tuesday. You managed to have this dream exactly— only for you it was a young woman, not a mother, and you managed to invent a feeling of longing and sadness.

They sat quietly in the room.

The claimant looked as though he might cry.

—I can't remember it properly, he said to himself.

—That feeling of longing and sadness, continued the examiner, is important. It is part of life's balance, to give things their proper worth. If a person was loved, and a person has died, we want to bring them with us while we still live, but we cannot allow their memory to ruin all new things. So, we must accord them a space of solemnity and reverence, and spontaneous joy in recollection. That is the exercise that we are trying to do with this dream. We are making a case for you to put your effort into. I want you to invent some memories that you might have had with this young woman and be lighthearted about it. She is, after all, not real. Since she is not real, you can play a bit. You can imagine that there were wonderful times, and that she has died, and that it was a tragedy the likes of which you could scarcely bear, but then—because it wasn't real, you can use it as a test case. You can be strong, and delight in all the fine things that you invent—all the fine things you did together. And you can imagine how a person might use this process to get over a difficult grief, and live a happy life.

—I remember, he said. I remember now that we talked about this. I think I do. I can remember thinking about her a lot, and I remember also, I remember . . .

—For now, said the examiner, let us think about another of the dreams I had that I gave to you. Do you remember the one where you worked in an antiques store—and you were always forgetting to lock the door. You were always leaving without locking the door?

—Yes, I remember that one.

—Well, do you remember that I did work in an antiques store, that I did forget to lock the door? And do you remember what happened?

—You were fired? You lost your position?

—No, nothing of the sort. I just went back in the middle of the night and locked the door. No one ever found out—not until I told you about it.

The claimant leaned back in his chair and took a deep breath.

—You want me to try to write this down?

—I know you can, said the examiner. Even if you haven't written before, or if you wrote once long ago, but have forgotten how. I'm sure you can do it.

The claimant leaned over the paper and began to write.

He wrote:

✛ ✛

I am in a train station. I am wearing a coat because it is winter. There are birds everywhere, and I am crying.

✛ ✛

—Very good, said the examiner. Very good! You see, you *can* write! And your handwriting is very clean and even. I am going to go out onto the porch so you can write in peace. Come out when you are ready.

The claimant sat and wrote, and it felt very good to him to write. He felt he could see them so clearly, the things he had dreamed, and that writing made them firm. The examiner was so kind to him. He tried to imagine her face as the face of the young woman. He tried to imagine her face looking out of a train window. He wrote and wrote, and when he went out on the porch and showed her, the examiner smiled and touched him on the arm and he sat beside her. In the night there had been a storm and part of the fence was down. He said, the fence has fallen down, and she said, if part of it has fallen down, it isn't a fence any longer. Then she said she was sorry, that that was a joke. And he thought about it as a joke, and soon they were sitting in the dusk.

—WHAT IS IT LIKE to be an examiner?

—It is difficult at first. One has to be so careful, always afraid of saying the wrong thing. It begins that you work with people who were not sick, who are not recovering. Everything else is the same, but the people you are working with are actors.

—Actors?

—People who are playing a part, who are pretending to be something they are not. And still others are watching the whole thing and keeping track. They grade you on your performance, and if you do well enough, you may be offered a position as an examiner. Of course, one is only an examiner D at that point.

—D?

—There are several ranks—D, C, B, A, and G. They have different levels of responsibility and autonomy.

—Teresa, what are you now?

—Examiners are not supposed to talk about this sort of thing.

—Oh, please!

—Examiner A.

—That is so wonderful!

He shook her arm with both his hands.

—I am so happy for you, he said. What a great thing to have done.

The examiner was taken aback. A pleased smile flashed on her features and was dispelled.

—Oh, it was nothing, she said. I just do my work and try as hard as I can.

—But still, he said. But still. Just imagine—me, getting an examiner A to help me! What a great thing.

—Anders, she said. A person always gets an examiner A at first—that's what they are for.

—But still, he said. I am sure that you are different from the other examiners. Don't you think you are? Don't you do things a bit differently? Are all examiners women?

—Yes, she said. They are all women.

—And are all gardeners men?

She laughed.

—Not at all. They can be either. And there are many men who work with examiners. It is only that—it has been found that women are better at this task.

—Could I become an examiner?

—You, an examiner? There are things like examiners—you could take a position like that, within this system. Indeed, many who come to us as claimants end up working in our ranks once they have recovered completely. It is a matter of how well your recovery proceeds. There are many things we do not know, many questions unanswered. We shall see what you are best suited for.

—I think that I might like it, he said. Sometimes I feel that we are a bit alike.

—It is good to feel that, she said. That is the feeling we talked about—empathy. It is what humans can feel for other humans. It is very natural.

—But I think we are alike, he said.

—We may be, she said. But feeling that we might be—that is what is most important.

THEY WERE STANDING before the pictures again. One was
a painting of a farm scene. Another was a photograph of a hill
with a hole in it.

—How many times, said the examiner, we have stood looking at
these pictures.

—There is someone in the cave, I think.

—Why do you think that, Anders?

—Because there is a line here, and here and here. I believe
that someone must have walked there, up the hill, again and
again and again until a path was worn down. If that is true,
then maybe the person is inside of the hill, in the cave, in this
photograph. I have often thought this when we have stood here,
but I wasn't ready to speak about it until now.

—Do you put someone there?

—What do you mean?

—Anders, do you put someone there, in the cave? Is there
someone you imagine to be there, when you imagine a person
in there?

He shifted his weight and the floor creaked slightly.

—I put you in there. It's you that is in there.

—That's all right. That's okay.

She patted him reassuringly.

—I am the only person you know. Of course, you would put me
in there. Who else would you put?

—It isn't for good, he said. I pictured you coming out, also.

She narrowed her eyes.

—Did you really?

—No. But, I can.

—Anders, she said. Just so you know, you can't say that something is *inside the hill*. A hill is a solid object. If a tunnel is bored through it, or a cave is there, the cave replaces the inside of the hill. Then, a person who is in a cave is in a cave that goes into a hill. They are not *in a hill*. In the same way, a tunnel that goes through a hill has no part that is *in* the hill, unless, of course, the tunnel collapses. Then, the person that was in the tunnel when it collapsed could be said to be inside the hill.

—I like this one less and less, said the claimant, pointing to the painting.

—Why is that?

—I think that it doesn't reflect how things are very well. I am concerned about it never having happened.

—So you prefer real things?

—I think so, I think. No, that's not it.

—There are many imagined things that are good, said the examiner, and many that I know you like.

—I think maybe it is false. There isn't any hope in it.

—It looks cheerful enough to me, said the examiner quietly.

—But, ah, mmm . . .

—You are right, you know, said the examiner. It is a bad piece of art, and that is because it is an imposture. The artist was elsewhere when it was made. It would be good to take it down or to throw it away, but I think,

She tilted her head.

—I think it will be good for it to stay as a reminder to you of this moment. Good work.

ONE DAY, SHE SAT DOWN with him on the porch steps outside the house. It was a very gray day. The clouds were low over their heads, and there was hardly any sun. In fact, the town looked different beneath this sky. The claimant said this to the examiner,

—How different the weather makes things. You almost wouldn't know the street to look at it.

—That reminds me, she said, of an exercise. It might be hard for you, on a day like today, to think of the way things usually are, and remember them, but I want you to. I want you to close your eyes, and give me an account of what you see as you leave the house and go down into the town.

—THE FIRST THING, the claimant said, is that I shut the gate.
As soon as I've done that, I'm standing in the road. The road
goes in two directions. I always go to the left. There is a house
opposite, and it is the same as our house. There is a house to
the left of that, and opposite it, a house to the right of our house.
There are, on our street, nineteen houses on each side, as we go
down into the town. At the base of the hill, there is a depression
where water sometimes gathers. That's on the right side of the
street. There is a shop with a chessboard set up in the window.
The pieces are not set up properly. The board has been turned
ninety degrees. The queens are not on their color. As you . . .

—That is enough for now, said the examiner quietly. You are
doing so well. You see so much, I would never have guessed.

—The next thing, said the claimant, is a shop with a sewing
machine. The same dress is always in the machine, as if it
is about to mended, but it never is. It is always waiting to be
mended.

ANOTHER DAY, and they went down the road in the other direction. For the first time, they turned right. They walked for a good long while. For this good while there were houses on both sides, and then there were just houses on one side, and then none—just fields and woods. They had a picnic with them, and when they came upon a large rock that was pleasantly placed beneath the shade of a tree, they decided to sit and eat.

—Do you remember what I said to you last night? That I said, today we will practice how it would be to meet a person? Are you ready to try?

—A real person?

The claimant looked about him to see if there was someone approaching, or any sign of anyone nearby, but there was none. It was just a beautiful autumn afternoon, with leaves falling, and birds passing now and then through the air and through the trees.

—This is practice. We would be practicing. Shall we try?

—All right.

—I'm going to go around that bend there. When I come back over, I will be a different person, someone you have never met. I want you to speak to me as if you don't know me, and as if you are simply a human being like any other, meeting someone for the first time. You might contrive some reason to speak to me. Or, perhaps, I will have a reason to speak to you. That is how it is in the world. Ready?

—I am.

The examiner jumped down from the rock and walked away. His eyes followed her as she walked with a certain light grace between the roots of trees and the tall grasses. Soon she was out of sight. A sudden shyness and fear rose in him. He gathered himself.

—WHY, HELLO.

The claimant looked at her. She was wearing some kind of coat over her clothes and a different hat. Her eyes were painted.

He thought about this, and tried to remember what she had looked like before. Had she been wearing those same clothes before . . .

She was saying something to him. He was supposed to be speaking to a new person, and she looked like a new person. She was saying,

—Do you know the way to Calistor Avenue?

I haven't been there, he said.

And then he was thinking that he had been there. It was the one by the lake, not around the lake, but you passed it there, he thought. He had remembered looking at the sign, seeing the name, and not trying to pronounce it. But when you pronounced it, that's how it came out. Calistor. When he looked up, the woman was gone.

Oh, dear. How had he done?

THE EXAMINER came back around the corner, looking just as she had at the outset.

—Anders, she said. Anders, Anders, Anders. That won't do at all.

He looked at the ground near his feet.

—You were very convincing, he said. I really felt that you didn't know me.

—It is hard, isn't it, said the examiner, to have someone look at you as if they don't know you—when you feel they do or should.

—I don't like it. I felt very . . .

—Alone?

—Yes, alone.

—Maybe, she said. It would be easier for you if it were actually someone else.

—I think so, he said.

—There is someone over there, down the way a bit. Why don't you walk down there and speak to them.

HE WALKED down the road a bit. Sure enough, up ahead, there was a little house, a sort of tollhouse, with a long plank that lowered to block the road.

A man appeared as he approached.

—Papers, said the man.

—Papers?

—I need to see them. I need your papers, said the man.

—I don't, I don't have any, said Anders.

The man started for the tollhouse, as if to take some action, and right then, the examiner came up from behind.

—It's all right, she said. He's with me.

The toll minder nodded, and sat down on the bench where he had been. To him it was suddenly as though they were not there.

The examiner put her arm around the claimant.

—Let's go back, she said. You did just fine.

—Why did he ignore us like that? the claimant asked.

—Oh, that's what people do. He was just returning to the little world he inhabits when no one's around. At certain conversational junctures it's perfectly fine to do that. What you need to do is discover where such junctures lie.

SHE WAS WRITING her report and sipping a glass of sherry. She had been leafing through a score of Stravinsky, and it leaned on the back of the writing desk, its fine black lines radiating outward as if to cover the room.

+ +

The claimant has recovered most general function. He can wash himself, dress himself, eat, drink, cook, and govern his natural hours, sleeping at regular times. He has a tendency to drift, and fall into confusion, and he cannot yet discriminate between what is real and what is not.

The integration appears to be working. He speaks to me of his memories as I have invoked them—that is, as my memories which I have seeded into his dreams. This provides him with a level of remove that may permit him some grace.

All the same, the nightmares continue unabated. Here is the text of the last two:

—— ——

Where the buses all end up, I have gone there, somehow I've ended up there. The bus drivers all leave their buses wherever they can. It is a large yard in a sort of depression, surrounded by trees. Perhaps it was once a sump. It is enormous, and the buses are everywhere. Many of them are out of service, or have been forever. They don't even have wheels. The bus drivers get out of their buses one by one as they arrive, I didn't see this, but I know it, they get out and they walk to a wall at the back of the yard and they all stand facing the wall with their noses nearly touching it. There are hundreds of them. It is how they sleep. I am one of the bus drivers. I pull my bus into the yard and stop it wherever I like. I get out. I walk slowly across the yard, as slowly as I like, and when I reach the wall, there is a place there, an empty spot, and I ease myself into it. I am so near the wall, I can feel the cold radiating from the stone. I am basking in that cold. I feel myself falling back into sleep.

✳

*I am driving again, this time I am driving a car, an open
car, in the countryside. There is someone beside me in the
car, but I cannot turn my head to look at her. We are going
tremendously fast, and the road is curved. We are moving
back and forth on the road, the wind is pushing us, and it
requires all of my skill just to continue. I want to turn my
head and look at her, but I cannot. The light is going out of
the countryside that I am in. The whole thing is going dim;
the sun is not seeing—it's more that, someone is closing her
eyes, and the light will soon be gone. Just as the light is gone,
I turn my head to look and I see her, there, she flashes briefly
in the dimness, and the car spills off the road, rolling and
rolling and rolling and my body is racked with pain.*

— —

*Yesterday, he woke confused; he had forgotten our speech
about his dreams. He told me that he wanted to go back to
where he had been. He named the city. He asked me if I
knew the way. I told him that I did know the way. He should
listen to me and follow my instructions. I led him through a
breathing exercise and he fell back into sleep and slept through
the morning. When he woke the second time, he remembered
nothing . . .*

✚ ✚

She paused in her writing. The claimant was stirring in the next
room.

—I'M HERE, she said.

—Rana, he said. Rana.

—There is no Rana.

—Rana. Where are you?

The claimant sat up in bed. His face was pallid. The window was wide open and the room was full of the night air. There was so much of it, it rolled back and forth over them. The examiner shut the window, and then they were there in the room again.

—I'm here, she said.

The claimant began to cry.

—In the last week, I didn't know, he said. I didn't know. She was sick and she hid it from me. I promise you, if I had known, I would have, I would have . . .

—Go back to sleep, said the examiner.

She knelt by him on the bed and eased him down into a sleeping position. He reached for her, and clutched at her arm, pulling her to him. She lay for a second against him, and his breathing, at first ragged, grew regular. She came out from under his hand, and left the room.

THE EXAMINER sat long into the night thinking. She did
not want to make this decision. She would delay it as long as
possible. If he were to be processed again . . . it pained her to
think of it. She remembered her first work, with a claimant who
had been processed three times. He could hardly speak. She had
taught him to take care of himself, and had helped him to learn
a simple vocation.

It wasn't that the process made the brain function less well.
It only removed a capacity for action. Each time, a person
became less likely to follow an intuition, or take up an idea or a
challenge. Those who lost all or nearly all of this *impulsiveness,*
as it was called, a reuse of the word, became the basic workers,
the deed-doers in the gentle villages. It was they whom one
saw through windows, people who would never go out of
themselves, or leave a house unbidden, it was they who stood
in simple uniforms, gardening or sweeping in the streets. They
were a staple of the gentle villages, a staple, a tool, a mechanism,
and its result.

Others, who could be helped with one processing—went on to
do what they liked. Such a person could return to regular life,
or stay within the system. Some, as she had told the claimant,
even became examiners. They never seemed to be bothered by
learning the methods—never seemed to guess that those same
methods might have been employed to alter their own minds. It
is only natural, supposed the examiner. In an extreme case,
I suppose, I might have even been . . .

She shuddered.

It was the nineteenth day. There was scarcely any time left.
When the sun rose, the examiner was still sitting where she
had been. Her eyes were open, and focused on some point on
the wallpaper. But which point it was, even she couldn't say.
Light had stood in the sky for an hour or two when she heard
something in the next room, a sort of battering, a crash, and
a low moan.

—ANDERS!

The bedroom and all its elements were overturned.

He must have lifted the bedframe up and knocked it over.
Was he asleep when he did it? The dresser was on its side. The
mattress was over him, bent practically in half. He was shaking,
curled in the corner under the mattress. She pulled it off of him.

—Anders!

The claimant looked at her strangely, as if she were mad.

—Who are you talking to? he said. Who is Anders? Where am I?

His voice was different—his inflections had changed. He looked
at her and it was as if he did not know her at all—as if he had
just appeared that moment, from some other place.

The examiner looked at him in horror. Be calm, be calm.

He had cut his hands badly, and the blood was smeared on his
face and chest. He looked up at her, and his face was wet. He
was crying, but he was angry.

—Anders! she said, I need you to calm down.

—Who are you? Who are you?

He burrowed his head into his arms, pushed himself into the
corner, and screwed his eyes shut.

—Anders! Anders!

He did not respond.

The examiner rushed from the room.

2

A BRIGHT LIGHT WOKE HIM. Something was shining through the window, and his face felt very hot. He rolled over and slowly looked around. He could scarcely manage it, but he looked around. His eyes failed him and drifted shut. He was curled in a quilt with the sheets in disarray.

The claimant lay in a bed that was set against a wall. A chair had been pulled up next to the bed. A chair had been pulled up, and there was someone in it.

It was an old woman. Her face creased in a smile.

The claimant squinted and struggled to open his eyes and see her.

She leaned her face in close to his, seeming to ctch his features into her mind.

His eyes shut and he slumped in the bed.

With a strength that belied her age, she pushed his body into a sleeping posture, and stepped away.

IT WAS A GOOD SITUATION, thought the examiner. He appears young and strong. He had woken remarkably soon after the shot—only eighteen hours, if the report was to be believed. The examiner had been at this job long enough to know that not all information was correct.

In fact, she thought, often it is wrong on purpose.

She busied herself making some tea. How should she start with this one?

The usual method? Or another approach? Lately she had been favoring the original way, the first way, although she had made her career with her unusual treatments. This time, she would stick to the original method. No speech until the claimant speaks. It was a measurement of sorts. The examiner believed very fervently in measurement.

She set the teapot down on the table and took a pen and paper off a shelf on the wall.

✚ ✚

Arrived in Gentlest Village P6.

Received claimant. He appears healthy and ready for treatment.

✚ ✚

THE TWO COULD BE SEEN through any window of the house, sitting together. He would sit in one chair and she would sit in another. They would sit for long hours, practically motionless.

Through another, they might be seen practicing skills. The old woman would mime the donning of clothes, and help him again and again and again to perform the basic tasks. No matter how he tried, the man could not button the buttons of his shirt. He failed again and again. But, if he was failing, the expression of the old woman seemed to say: This, what we are doing, it is the hardest thing in the world. No one has ever done it. No one until you. And now it has fallen to you to try. Let us try. Let us try again.

One could see them practicing the use of the stairwell, a thing to which one clung with both arms, while lowering leg after leg up and down. It was used for getting to and fro—for going from the top of the house to the bottom.

One could see the man standing in a tub while the old woman poured water over him and scrubbed and scrubbed until he was clean. And soon, he had learned to scrub as well. Soon, he could do it by himself.

If one waited some days and looked through the bottom windows, a different scene might present itself. The two sat at a long table, and blocks with pictures of things were passed back and forth. Large bound sheets full of pictures were shown and shared.

Sometimes a task would be terribly difficult—terribly, terribly difficult, and the man would cry. He would sit down on the floor and cry. Then the old woman would sit down beside him on the floor and wait, and when he was done crying, they would try again.

Her patience was the heart of it. She was as patient as a person could be.

THE HOUSE was a tall Victorian house. That meant it was nicely made, and with good proportions. The rooms had high ceilings. The windows were large and bore many panes within their cavities. The floors had long wooden boards that ran the length of each room. Many were covered with fine carpets. When a person trod on the floors, the boards creaked, and in this way the house was a little bit alive.

Along the stairs there were photographs. At each step there was another photograph. By walking up and down the stairs one could find a sort of history—but of what it was hard to say. There were many photographs of machines. Winged machines, wheeled machines, farm machines. There were many people with somber clothing and blurry faces. Sometimes there were many people together in one photograph, and when there were, they usually all stood facing in the same direction. How could the photographer stand in front of them—so many, and not be noticed?

The banister was of a swooping brown wood and felt very pleasant under the hand. One could run the hand along it, all the way down the stairs, and then one would be at the bottom. All the way from the top to the bottom.

The bottom of the stairs faced a long, narrow hall—and at its end a door that was never open. This door was set with colored glass of every sort. It would be a nice place to lie, to lie flat on the back in the hall and be covered with the colored light.

There were two paintings in this hall—one of a bird with long feathers, and another of a woman who wore clothing that made her look very much like a bird. She was angry, and her face was cruel, and she filled the area around the door with her anger.

Many of the windows in the house had seats in them. The seats were covered in cushions, and a person could sit there as long as they liked. Eventually, the sun might become blinding. Or, the sky would become dark. Then it would be time to go to a different place.

The woman who walked about in the house was very old. She was always watching everything that happened, and always listening. She was a comfort because she would be there in an instant to help, or she would wait for hours until the next time she should be there in an instant to help. She wore dark stockings of wool and no shoes. Her clothes were the same color as the walls.

The kitchen was the airiest room in the house. It had many windows, and they looked out on a garden full of plants. Some things from the garden would end up in the kitchen. There were many times when one could leave the kitchen happily, and one would often come into it with great happiness, too. The kitchen was the best room in the house.

There were many places in the house for putting things. One could put things from one place to another, and they would go back to the place they had been before. This was a sort of game. As many times as one would do it, the things would return. Even paintings that were tilted, or hairs placed under small statues.

The man would get up and go to the stairs at first, and he would wait there, and wait until she came and then they would go down the stairs together. Or, later, he would go down sitting, go down sitting all the way. He had a hard time making his legs and arms work like the old woman could. Whenever she wanted to do something, she did it.

Finally, he could go down the stairs just like her. In fact, he could go down faster than that. He would go down the stairs and the old woman would find him and they would have things to do all day and then it would be time to sleep.

Whenever he didn't have things to do, the old woman found something for him to do. But when he had something to do, she was never there.

The man liked the pants that he wore, and there was a day when he put all the clothes on by himself and came down the stairs by himself, and worked on a thing he had decided to do by himself and ate by himself and it was not until the evening that he saw her. Then they sat on the closed porch and she lit a candle and it was a sort of celebration.

AND ON THE SEVENTIETH DAY, the man spoke.

—CAN I, the water.

The examiner sat quietly looking at the claimant. She said nothing.

—Can you give me the water?

His words were clear and distinct.

She picked up the pitcher of water with both hands and gravely presented it to him.

—Here you are, she said.

—Thank you, said the claimant.

The examiner nodded and went back to what she had been doing as if nothing remarkable at all had just happened.

SHE DID NOT begin to speak to him until two days had passed. Until then, she would answer him when he spoke, and speak to confirm the sense of what he had done.

But, when she began, she spoke with full diction and clarity.

—I am the examiner, she said. It is my purpose to help you. I have no purpose but that. I live here in this house. This house is the place where you live. We live in this house together. We are together in completing something. The thing that we are completing is your recovery. You were very sick. You were totally incapacitated by an illness. You almost died. When you were on the point of death, you were rescued, and now you are being brought back to health. There is every reason to have real optimism about your chances. I feel certain that things will go well for you, and though you do not know what lies ahead, you may rely on me.

—Where . . .

He swallowed.

—Where are we?

—We are in the house where we live. Where else would we be? How could it be possible to be anywhere else but where we are? How silly.

—How do you know me?

—I am the person who knows you. I am the only one. And you, you know me. We create a world through that, through knowing one another. You need not worry yourself about that. We have this house that we live in, and in it we do the things we need to do to live. We cook and eat, we clean ourselves, we practice our tasks. You will have many tasks to learn and do.

—I feel, I feel very sad.

—It isn't sadness that you feel. Sadness is a feeling of loss. There is something one wanted, and one doesn't have it—or there is a way one wanted things to be, and things aren't that way. That is sadness. Instead, you feel rootlessness. You have not attached yourself to the things around you. By doing so, you will find that your happiness can grow.

She led him over to a wall.

—Let us begin here. What do you see?

—Two, two . . .

—Pictures. They are called pictures. But you knew that. You know many words. They will return to you soon enough. Let us try—what is the top one called? What sort of picture is it?

—A painting.

—That's right. And the bottom one?

—A picture.

—It is a picture, but what sort?

—A photograph.

—That's right. Tell me about these pictures.

The man looked at the pictures for a very long time. After he had done so, he went and sat back down in the dining room with his head in his hands. The old woman followed him and sat beside him, with one hand on his shoulder. The rest of the day, they spoke very little, and whenever he looked up, her eyes were there, hard upon his, full of reassurance and strength.

THE NEXT DAY, she led him back to that wall.

—Tell me about these pictures, she said.

He looked at them and looked at them. Then he went into the dining room. There was a pad of paper there, and a pen. The old woman had left it there, in the middle of the table, and said nothing about it.

The man took the pad and began to draw. He drew and drew. An hour passed. He looked up. He had done a very rudimentary drawing of a farmhand feeding some chickens. With some difficulty one could perceive that that is what it was.

The old woman came over.

—Very good, she said, very good. I think . . .

She went into the kitchen and then came again and stood by him.

—In fact, I am sure of it. I like yours more. Sometimes sketches of things are to be preferred to paintings. I find that I often prefer artists' sketchbooks. Such books are like this—

She drew a notebook from the wall, a loose leather fold with blank paper stitched into it. A pencil was tied to a string that hung from the side.

—You can have this one, she said. Draw in it as much as you like.

He took the book under his arm and sat intently in the chair, looking at nothing insomuch as he was looking at anything.

ONE DAY, the claimant began to write things down. He wrote
things on the paper in between his drawings. The writing
was not involved. He would write, This is a drawing, or, This
is an idea for a drawing, or, A dog, or, The third one like this.
Whenever he used the paper, he tore it out of the notebook and
put it in a pile. The examiner never read any of his writing while
he was awake, but in the night, she went through the pile of his
drawings, very slowly and meticulously, missing nothing.

From these drawings, she learned many things. For instance, he
had been in a gentlest village before. This did not surprise her
in the slightest.

I wonder, she thought, which of my fellow examiners dealt with
him?

Of course, she did not know all of the examiners. In fact, she
knew but a tiny sliver of the total number. And if the news was
to be believed, the Process of Villages was growing all the time.
Soon, it would be everywhere.

She sat at the table, turning over the drawings one at a time.
There was a drawing of a tower, and of a bird. These were
imitations from children's books she had shown him. In her
mind's eye she could see the originals.

But here was one she had not seen. It was a drawing of a room,
and in the room there was a bed. It looked almost like a coffin.
A woman lay in it, with her eyes shut and her hands folded. He
had crossed out the woman repeatedly, but she could still be
made out.

The old woman flipped through the sheets from the previous
day. Another—the same image, with the woman crossed out.
Another, and another, and another. He had been drawing all
afternoon. All afternoon, he had drawn this same scene and
crossed it out. There was no text with any of these.

She put the drawings back exactly where they had been and
went upstairs to write her report.

—SOMETIMES I WILL TELL YOU STORIES, said the examiner. They may be full of things that you do not understand. That is not important. It isn't important that you understand what I say. What's important is that you behave as a human being should when someone is telling a story. So, listen properly, make noises at appropriate times, and enjoy the fact that I am speaking to you. If it is your turn to tell a story, remember that it is not very important that you are understood as long as you give the person the happiness of being told a story, and of being near you while listening to a story. Much of the speech we do is largely meaningless and is just meant to communicate and validate small emotional contracts. Are you ready?

The claimant waited to see if she was done talking and then he nodded slowly.

—We shall go for a walk and during the walk I will suddenly begin a story. Will you know how to act?

—We shall go for a walk, she repeated. During the walk, I will suddenly begin a story. Will you know how to act?

—WHEN I WAS A YOUNG WOMAN, she said to the claimant,
I lived a very wild life.

He sat beside her in the square at the center of the town. There
was a carousel, and they sat on its edge, leaning on the poles
from which rose the horses, the carriages, the leaping fish.

—Oh, I could tell you, she said, a story or two from that time. I
had an old uncle who had fought in a war. Did we speak about
that? People killing each other for land or money? Yes? War.
Anyway, this was before the republic, so there were still wars.
He said he and his fellow soldiers were set to guard a road. So,
that is—anyone who came down the road was to be killed. They
had tools, guns, with which to do it. Well, there was a general
who was trying to escape the province. Apparently he had been
hemmed in, and was surrounded. They were intent on capturing
him. Anyway, they were sitting there at the crossroads, and it was
a hot day, and they were feeling a bit sleepy, and a man comes
down the road out of the distance, a fiddler, playing away as he
walks. He comes right up to them, a real ragamuffin, and plays
for them awhile. Then off he goes on up the road. Thing is—the
next day, the orders come down for the general's capture, and
they include a picture of him. Guess what?

The old woman slapped her leg.

—The fiddler was the general. He had put on some old clothes
and used a musical talent everyone had forgotten he had. Thing
is—my uncle and his fellow soldiers were petrified. They
figured the news of his escape would come out and they'd all be
court-martialed. But it didn't happen that way.

—How did it happen?

—How did what happen?

—Things—how did they go?

—Oh, ha, well, no one ever heard of the general again. So, here's
my opinion. I think the general found out that it was a better

life being an itinerant fiddler than it was being a general, and I think he didn't want to go back.

The claimant thought about that for a while.

—Anyway, said the old woman, I always consider that, I always do, whenever I try out a new role, or put on some costume, even if it's just a new way of thinking about something. There are some doors—when you go through them, they close behind you.

In the square, it was becoming dark. The claimant liked the carousel, and so, he and the examiner would go there every evening. Every afternoon when the sun was by the trees, they would walk down, and they would sit there talking until the lights were on in all the houses and the street lamps were pulsing. Then they would walk back along the street and look into the houses. Sometimes they would see people inside, and they would talk about them, and about how their lives seemed.

The claimant had been surprised to see that there was only ever one person in any given house. None of the people ever went beyond the fence that surrounded each house, and he never saw them speaking or calling out. The examiner said that it was natural. There are people, she said, who require no more than that it rains sometimes.

He asked her if it was like this everywhere. To that, she replied, where is this everywhere? And when he had been quiet for a while, she said, there are many places where people live together with other people. It is to a place like that—it's to such a place you are headed.

ONE DAY, the examiner came into the claimant's room as he was turning down the lamp.

—Shall I tell you about tomorrow, she asked.

—Please.

—Tomorrow we will wake. You will wake and I will wake. You will dress and I will dress. We will convene downstairs in the kitchen, and whoever is there first will put the kettle on to boil. We will sit and listen for the kettle, and make tea, and have some small breakfast. Then we will go out on the porch, where a great business will occur. Tomorrow, we shall speak about names.

—Names?

—For now, I will say no more, save this: think as you go off to sleep—why does any thing have any particular name?

—NAMES, SAID THE EXAMINER. Names. What is this?

—A spoon.

—And this?

—A shoe.

—And what of me?

—You are the examiner.

—Is that my name?

The claimant waited.

—What is your name? she asked.

—I don't have a name.

—You once had a name, she said. When you were sick, you had a name. But that name was forfeited—given up. Now you shall have a new name, but not a real name, a practice name. Do you know why you shall have a practice name? It is because tomorrow we shall go to another village. We are going to live in a new place, and there you will meet people.

She saw his expression change, and altered her tone.

—Oh, don't worry about that. You are concerned. You have become tied to this house, is that it?

He nodded.

—Well, what if I were to tell you that we have already moved twice in the time that I have known you? What if I were to tell you that this is the third village we have been in—and now we are going to the fourth?

—The third? But . . .

—In the first village, there was just a house. The first village is just a single house. When we were there, we never left. It is called the gentlest village, because it is a house, and everything that can be seen from that house. The second village was the place from which we walked out one day. You may remember it—you picked a daisy and cried when I told you that you'd killed it. Then we put it in a vase in the kitchen and it lived for a week very beautifully before shriveling to nothing. Do you remember that?

He nodded.

—Well, in that place, you recall, we occasionally saw a person through a window. How is it that things are here?

—We see people through windows, and in the yards.

—That's so. And do you not see that there are many many more people than there were before?

He nodded.

—Even, once, he said, I spoke to someone.

—You did, she said. You approached one of the gardeners where he was working, and you spoke out loud to him. Do you remember what happened then?

—He didn't reply.

—No, he didn't, he couldn't reply. He was a person who no longer wants to speak. His labor is enough for him. But, listen. In the next village, the people you speak to, they will speak back to you. But, listen, she said again. This is how it will be in the next village: you shall be called Martin Rueger. That is your name. It is not your final name. It is a name for you to wear like a fine new coat. If it is ill suited, or if you spoil it, we shall go to another place and try again with another name. We are testing the waters and learning things. We are learning how you may do with others. Do you see?

—Martin, he said. Martin Rueger. It is a good name. And . . .

—Yes?

—What is your name?

—For now it will be Emma Moran.

—If someone looks like me, does that mean it is likely their name . . .

He sat a moment, working the thought out in his head.

—Does it mean their name will be somewhat like mine? Like spoons or knives?

—Each person has a name. The point of it is this—to make it easier to talk about things, especially things that aren't present. Names are much less important than people think. They aren't really important at all. You and I get by for instance most of the time without talking at all—isn't that so?

The claimant nodded.

—But for you, it is a very nice thing now, to receive a name. That's because it is the occasion of our move to a new village where you will meet other people. The name is a symbol of your progress.

—How will I remember it?

—I will remember it for you—just point to your ear if you want me to use it in a sentence.

3

THE EXAMINER and the claimant were sitting in a room. It was a large room, a sort of town hall. There were some tables with food on them. There was a band set up at one end playing music. There were some couples dancing. On one side of the claimant there was a large fat man who had said a few things out loud to the claimant. The claimant had not said anything back. The man was using suspenders on his pants, and the claimant was having some thought about suspenders, and also trying to stay as near to the wall as possible. The examiner would tap his chair occasionally to remind him that she was there.

In fact, right at that moment, two people were standing in front of them. A man and a woman were standing there. The man was about the same age as the claimant, and the woman was younger. They were both very handsome. The man's arms and legs were strong and his hair was very full. The woman was very slender and her face had many possibilities. Looking at her, one could imagine many scenes.

These people had been standing there some time. The examiner was speaking to them.

At some point, the claimant realized that they had been addressing him. Many of the questions had been directed at him. The conversation had been going on for some time, and he had been failing to be a part of it.

At that moment, the old woman tapped his chair and the conversation began again from the beginning.

—Hello, said the claimant.

—Martin, said the young woman, I believe we met before, the other day in the market? Do you remember my name?

The claimant looked at her.

—It's Hilda. Hilda.

She repeated it and her tongue leapt off the *a* of *Hilda* in a pleasing sort of way.

—Hilda, he said.

—That's right. And this is Martin, my husband.

The claimant looked at Martin in confusion.

—Yes, said Martin, we have the same name. Sort of a coincidence, I'd say.

He reached out and shook the claimant's hand. This shaking of hands was strange but pleasant. When the man had taken his hand back, Martin reached out and took it again to shake it some more. He shook it a bit and everyone laughed.

—You see, said Hilda, it made it easy for me to remember your name. All I have to do is remember, *Martin,* and I have two places to use it. I can use it for you, she said, indicating the claimant, and for you, smiling at the man.

—But there are so few Hildas, said her husband. I don't get much use out of your name.

—Stop it, you! she said.

She kissed her husband on the cheek.

The claimant looked away in embarrassment.

Then the examiner was tapping his chair. He looked up.

Martin repeated the question he had been asking.

—Do you like fishing?

—I don't know.

—Doesn't know if he likes fishing, well. Well. If you do, or if you want to find out—you can come along. I go out most weekends, early in the day—just in a rowboat on the lake. You're welcome to come, be assured. Twenty-three Juniper Lane. Just knock on the door some day, Martin Rueger, and tell us you'd like to go fishing.

The claimant felt he was still looking at them. He was thinking about the conversation and what he would say next, but then he looked up and he realized they had gone. They had been gone for some time.

—Come now, Martin, said the examiner. Let's go home.

THEY SAT ON THE STAIRS side by side looking down. Although they had moved houses, the house was the same. The same photographs ran down the left wall. He could close his eyes and see them.

The aviator with his goggles in his hand, standing by a plane.

The family with poodle partially hidden behind a tree.

The girl as if on her first day of school.

The long lawn where sun had blighted the grass and the edge of the photograph was burned.

He often thought about that one.

—We have many things to discuss, said the examiner.

The claimant moved his toes back and forth against the step.

—Have you begun to think of yourself as Martin? she asked.

—No. Not until today.

—And was it strange, did you feel it was strange, having that woman speak to you in that way?

—They are married—she and the man?

—They are married and live together. Do you know what that means?

—It means that they are for each other, they possess each other. It means people should leave them alone and not interfere?

—It does not mean that. Some people would like it to. It means that they have declared, that each has declared that the other is of great importance to him or her. Life is life. It is not the sets of rules people make. If someone were to fall in love with that man

and he were to fall in love with her, he would very likely go off
and leave that woman, Hilda. And the same is true of Hilda. All
bonds are conditional. It is important to remember that. Why is
it? Why is it important to remember that?

—I don't know.

—It is important because if you expect that such bonds are
permanent, then you can do yourself harm when it becomes
true that the bonds are not. Do you see that? The most realistic
view is the safest. That is the view we take here.

—But if I were to spend time with Hilda . . .

—Her husband might not like it. He would probably try to
stop you, and stop her from doing that. But, what will happen
will happen. You have to be calm about everything and
understand—in this life all things that may happen do.

They sat for a while.

—It might be comfortable for you, said the examiner, to have
a cover story of some sort, a way of talking about how you spend
your time and why you are here. Would you like that? Should
we prepare one?

The claimant nodded.

—All right, Martin. What is the story that includes Martin
and Emma and speaks to why they live in this house and why
they go about in this town? It should be the simplest possible
explanation. Do you know that law? The simplest explanation
is always the correct one?

The claimant shook his head.

They sat for a while.

—Maybe you are studying something and I am your assistant,
he said.

—What could I be studying? she asked.

—These villages, he said. Maybe you are studying them. Maybe I am your helper. I am going through them and through studying me, you are studying them.

—Ha.

The examiner laughed.

—Don't you think that is a bit too close to the truth? How about I am studying plants. I am drawing plants. We will set up a station in the house where we will lay out and press plants and we will draw them. You enjoy drawing. We can work together on this. You can take your book around and draw plants in other places. We can collect plants. It will be very useful to us.

—Can you draw a plant, Emma?

She smiled.

—We shall see.

—Now?

—All right.

THEY WENT DOWNSTAIRS and into the dining room. The examiner took out a large sheet of paper and laid it across the dining room table. She brought out some pencils of various thicknesses, and a sprig of thyme from the kitchen. She laid it on the paper and sat looking at it.

The claimant watched her. He held his hand as if he were holding the pencil she was holding.

She leaned over the table and began to draw. With quick, precise strokes, she sketched out the thyme plant. When she was partway through, she stood up and went outside. In a moment, she was back, and she was holding a whole thyme plant. She washed it in the sink, dried it with a cloth, and came and laid it on the table.

—Now, I can draw the roots, she said.

She went then to her task, switching pencils often, and pausing to sharpen them. The claimant watched in wonder as the plant emerged on the page, very delicately. So delicately!

And then she was done.

—How could you do that? asked the claimant. How is that? How could it be?

—Do you remember which one of us suggested that I draw plants?

He shook his head.

—Well, I suggested it. That makes it very plausible that it is something I could do. You see how it is now? I wouldn't have suggested something I couldn't do . . . isn't that true?

The claimant smiled.

—And you will teach me.

—Yes, she said. It will be a good thing for us.

23 JUNIPER LANE

The claimant and the examiner approached the house. It was precisely the same as the house they lived in, so it was very comfortable to stand there in the doorway. Surprises—there never would be any!

The door opened, and Hilda was standing there. She was wearing a short yellow dress in honor of the springtime.

—Good evening, she said. Come in, come in!

Her eyes met Martin's and traveled over them and into them. He wondered if it had really happened or if he was imagining it. I am imagining it, he decided. It is because of what I was told.

They went into the hall and passed between the pheasant painting and the painting of the angry woman. They went to a closet and hung their coats. They were led through the passage to the dining room, and sat at the same table where the claimant had spent so much time.

—Martin will be back in a moment, said Hilda. He just ran down to the market to get some salmon for the salad.

She set out on the table a tray with some drinks.

—Here you are, Emma, and this is for you, Martin.

She left the room, then popped her head back in.

—Oh, Martin, she said, could you help me with something?

HE CAME INTO THE KITCHEN and she was standing in a sort of pose, facing him, her shoulders askance. Her eyes were wide open and she was looking right at him. He could hardly bear it.

She stepped close to him and went up on her tiptoes to whisper something in his ear.

—I need to speak to you.

He could feel the length of her against his arm. The buttons on her dress pressed into his skin. That's how close she stood.

—I need, can we meet in private?—When?

—Leave your house in the middle of the night, not tonight, but tomorrow. I'll be outside in the street, and we can go somewhere to speak. Right after the clock strikes one.

Should he agree?

He nodded.

—WELL, WELL, WELL, said Martin. Well, well, well. This was a fine supper after all. I thought it would be just a disaster, but that market down in the square, why, it saves the day every time. You wouldn't expect such a small market to have the things you need—but it is almost like they contrive to have only those things. The things you don't need, they don't have. The things you need, they have. What an idea! Why don't all markets work that way?

Emma chuckled to herself.

—They must know you very well, she said. Maybe when they see you enter the store, they put out items just for you.

—If it's true, said Martin, I should pay them double. What a great place this is.

He winked at the claimant. When the claimant returned his gaze, he indicated the next room with his head.

The claimant looked around. No one else had seen.

—I'm going to get a start on these dishes, said Martin.

He stood up and started collecting the plates. When Hilda got up, too, he shook his head.

—You cook, I clean, I cook, you clean. You know the rules. Fair is fair.

—I'll help you, said the claimant.

—Now that's some help I'll accept.

The two men went into the next room.

HE MOTIONED MARTIN OVER to the far side, and shut the door to the kitchen.

—Do you know how Hilda and me got here?

—No, you've never said.

—As I understand it, this village is actually part of the Process of Villages. Hard to believe, but true, as far as it goes. In any case, just to get in, you have to take some examinations and prove that you are a decent enough person not to disturb anything. I'll tell you a secret.

The man leaned in.

—Hilda didn't pass.

The claimant looked at him in shock.

—But . . .

—Yes, she didn't pass. Apparently she lies, and she is given to, what did they call it, precipitous actions.

—What was the test like?

—It was a week-long monitoring. You stay at a house and they watch you and send people to speak to you. After a while, they learn enough about you to make a decision.

—Did you pass?

—Of course I passed! You know me now, can you imagine I wouldn't have passed?

—I didn't say that, I just. Maybe it is a hard test.

—Oh no, it is easy. The easiest thing in the world. You would pass in a minute. But Hilda, well, she is a very odd young woman. It was her idea, too, to come here. She wanted to live in one of these so-called settled villages. She said the shapes were calm and comfortable. I said, the shapes of what. She said, all the shapes, the way everything there is better. So, here we are.

—But,

the claimant mulled for a moment.

—But, if she failed.

—I paid the man a large sum of money to look the other way.

The claimant turned his face away. He could scarcely believe it. He wanted to go back to the house immediately, but he felt he would be seen through. And so they sat there, quiet, for perhaps fifteen minutes.

—These fine spring days, said Martin. I could live like this forever. And I suppose we will, eh, friend?

He clapped the claimant on the back.

—I was just thinking, if you didn't take the test, you must have come here before they started the test. Is that so? You must have been around here quite a while. You must know this little village backward and forward.

—When did they start the test?

—I don't know—but these sorts of things, they always come up as soon as I'm the next one in line. Wouldn't surprise me at all if they started giving them the week before we came.

Martin put rubber gloves onto his hands and turned the faucet on, twisting the hot-water knob as far as it would go. The water poured out and steam rose to the ceiling. It was blisteringly hot, but Martin didn't flinch at all. He took each plate and thrust it into the water, without any concern for the spray. The water flushed the dishes of any and all debris. When that had been done, Martin gripped them, one by one, and scoured them

with a soapy rag. As he finished each, he would hand it to
the claimant, to dry and put away. The first dish the claimant
received was so hot he could scarcely hold it, but he did, and he
dried it with a soft white cloth and set it in the bureau behind
him. In the bureau there sat row after row of perfect white
plates, perfect white dishes, perfect white bowls, cups, teacups.
Things of every sort were there, and it was just as it had always
been. Every time that the claimant had opened such a drawer,
the inside had been just the same. He loved to look at these rows
of clean dishes. Why, he could . . .

—Martin Rueger! Another dish for you. Don't fail me now!

The claimant wondered what Martin would tell him. He
wondered why he had been brought into the kitchen. But it
soon became apparent that it was just for his company—for
that alone. This was an interesting idea, and one that he did not
entirely understand.

Or, it wasn't that he didn't understand it, he decided. It was that
he distrusted it. The examiner always said, distrust things that
are too easy. One wants the struggle—one shouldn't permit it to
be removed.

When they had finished the dishes, Martin showed the claimant
a special knife that they had brought with them for cutting fish.
It was very thin and the claimant found it a bit terrifying.

—This is a filet knife. I have used it to cut many fish. If you
were to pile all the fish that I have used this knife on, they would
fill this room and more. You literally could not fit them in this
room, not even considering their slipperiness. Even imagining
that they could be easily stacked, they still would not fit. If I
were to begin cutting them into tidy portions for meals today,
I would almost never be done. A week from now—after a week
of cutting, I would have cut just the smallest portion.

—You see, he continued, I used to work in a fish market. My
father was a fisherman, and all my uncles. But, they wanted
something else for me.

The claimant went back into the dining room.

—I can't bear to eat fish, Hilda was saying. I just, I think of them swimming around and looking forward to seeing the sunlight on the surface of the water, and then my heart goes out to them.

—Oh, that's rubbish, said Martin, coming up behind the claimant.

The two men sat down.

—For one, said Martin, the fish don't really care very much about the sunlight. I mean, you would, if we stuck you in the water, but they don't. And the other thing is—you love fish! You eat it all the time—and you even ask for us to have it when we haven't had it for a week or so.

—He's completely right, said Hilda. I was just talking about not liking fish. A person can do that, right? Talk about something, about not liking something. That's okay, isn't it?

—A person can talk about anything, as far as I'm concerned, said the examiner. That's the world we live in.

—Did you like the fish, Martin Rueger? Hilda asked the claimant.

—I liked it very much. This liquid that you poured . . .

—The lemon-butter sauce, yes, yes, it is my father's recipe, said Hilda. Of course, he didn't have to be a genius to think of it. It is just butter with lemon.

And in this way the conversation continued, both trivially and gravely, on into the night. When they retired, the claimant had so much to say about it all to the examiner that he couldn't decide what to say, and they walked all the way home in silence and in silence went to bed.

THE NEXT DAY they were occupied in collecting, pressing, and drawing specimens of plants, and there was no opportunity to talk more. Soon, it was the nighttime. Soon, the bell had struck midnight, and soon the bell had struck one.

The claimant got quietly out of bed. He had not taken off his trousers or shirt, and so it was but a simple matter for him to slip out of the room and down the stairs. Through the half-open door, he could see the examiner in her study. She sat at a desk with her back to him, writing long into the night as she always did. The light from the fixture in that room was shabby. It fell very bitterly over the room, and some of the light from a lamp in the street contested with it. The effect was: as she sat at her desk she looked like a figure in a woodcut. And she was as still. If she noticed his going, she made no motion to mark it.

Down the stairs and out the door he went, and then he was standing in the street.

.

—MARTIN!

Hilda was there. She was standing at the gate of a house, three doors down. He almost wouldn't have recognized her.

—I look very different, don't I? she asked. I can see it in your eyes. You thought that the person you were going to meet was just like Hilda, the Hilda you knew. And then here there is this other person standing on the street looking at you. She snuck out of her house at night to come and see you and you don't know why. Now you don't even know who this person is, but you can't stop looking at her.

She stepped closer, right up to him.

—Come along, there is a good spot for us this way.

As they made their way down the street, the claimant had a terrible feeling—that at every window there was a face, and that every face was turned to him, and that they all knew him, they all knew why he was there, and what he wanted.

But even he did not know what he wanted.

THEY WERE IN A HOUSE that was being built. She had taken
him to the edge of the town, and there, in the skeleton of a
house, she took his hand and sat him down.

—I want you to prove to me, she said. I want you to prove to me
that you are not an examiner, that you aren't part of this Process
of Villages! I am sure that something is amiss. They have been
doing terrible things to me. I have tried to escape several times,
but still they keep me here. First there was a different man, then
there was a woman. Now I am forced to live with Martin. He is
not my husband. I didn't even meet him until last week!

She pulled him to her.

—Oh, I know you are not one of them. I know that Emma is
your examiner. I can tell these things. I know that you will
help me.

She told him that she had woken in a house like the one she
lived in, that she had realized immediately she must pretend
to be recuperating. She said she had done so, and had passed
from one village to another. They move you in the night, she
said, while you are sleeping. She said they didn't think you
could remember anything, at first, and so they were constantly
changing their stories. She hardly slept once for a week straight,
she lay in bed with her eyes closed, just in order to see what
was happening, and she had discovered remarkable things.
They come in the night—people come into the house. They
put everything back. All through the house, they put things
back the way they were. And someone goes into the study and
unlocks the desk and takes things out.

—Do you know, she said, that they have a map, a sort of atlas,
of your entire life, of the life that you lived before you came
here? There is a place in the house where they keep it, and they
consult it—they use it to plan the way in which they will control
you. I know because it says so in the book. It mentions this
atlas specifically. But no matter where I looked in the house, I
couldn't find it.

She began to cry.

—I have tried so hard to remember my previous life. I have stared and stared into walls, carpets, clouds, desperately trying to conjure up anything, but it will not come. They took it all away.

He ran his hand up and down her back. It felt very good. Her hair was very soft and he was touching it. She was talking and talking and the skin of her face was soft and smooth. Her eyes were greedy and bright and full of need. She looked into his eyes as he thought no one ever had, and then first slowly and then desperately, they moved into each other, convulsing and shuddering in joy. She could hardly bear to stop talking long enough to kiss him, but then she did. It was almost too much to have her touch him, but as soon as she had, he could bear nothing else. It was the same with her. He could feel in her that it was the same with her, that they were mirroring each other, that their feelings were springing back and forth. And she kept saying, over and over—be true to me. Be true to me.

The claimant sat on the porch with the examiner. She was telling him about the weather and how the weather worked. He asked why the seasons could be the same for so long. He said it was contrary to what she had told him about seasons. She laughed and said, we have moved villages four times. How close together do you believe those villages to be? And she had explained that in the first village where they had been, it was winter.

—The villages are all over. Thus, we can go to whatever season we like, and live the same life.

She was talking now about the clouds, and naming all the kinds of clouds.

Meanwhile, he remembered what Hilda had said to him when she left:

—Meet me, not tomorrow night, nor the next night—but three nights from now. Come to my house, Martin will be away. He will be away. Tell no one!

THE NEXT DAY, it was all he could do to behave the same
as before. He felt when he saw the examiner that she would
see right through him, and so when he had left Hilda, he had
immediately made a plan. This was the first real action of his
new life. Making a plan: he hadn't done such a thing before.
What did it mean to be able to do such a thing?

When he had gotten home in the night, he brought with him
some new plants that he had found on the road. He sat up late
drawing them and tried harder than he ever had before, and he
managed a good drawing—the first good drawing he had done.

In the morning he showed this drawing to her.

She will think I am happy because I have succeeded. She will
attribute all my happiness to this.

AGAIN AND AGAIN, he found himself imagining Hilda. He pictured her lithe brown body with no clothing. He imagined her thinking of him, and he felt concern. Could it not be that she might discover that he was not worth knowing? Could she not feel she was better alone? He grew terrified. He was a failure. He had little to say—and had done nothing, knew nothing. The examiner was constantly pointing out his faults and his stupidity. And when the examiner praised him, it was only out of kindness. What was there about him that could equal up to Hilda?

He looked back on the supper at her house, and he thought of the way she had been looking at him. Again and again, he replayed in his mind the episode in the kitchen. He could see her standing askance before him. How he wanted to see her again!

The examiner had stopped speaking. She was sitting silently, looking over at him, and there was nothing in her eyes at all. She was just a husk, just patience itself. She would inhabit her body again when there was a reason to. In the meantime, she waited in some nearby place. That was almost how it was with her.

—EMMA, SAID THE CLAIMANT. I am ready to try again.

—Are you ready, she said.

—I am.

—To a meeting? To meet more people? You have been very quiet lately.

—I don't think that I was very good, when we met that couple. Or when we saw them again. I need to try harder.

—It isn't about trying, said the examiner. It is about being present. You are far inside yourself, and need to be at your edges, ready to spring.

—I will do it, he said. I will.

The examiner looked at the newspaper and saw that there was a meeting of a botanical society that very night.

—Who knew, she said. A botanical society.

—Oh, you must have known, said the claimant sharply.

The examiner raised an eyebrow, but said nothing.

THE BOTANICAL SOCIETY meeting was held in a building called the library. The claimant had not been to the library before, but he knew the word. It was a place for books to be kept, and indeed, when they arrived, it was quite full of books. This botanical society did not have very many plants or flowers. In fact, they were a sort of bibliographical botanical society, because mostly they talked about flowers and showed each other pictures of flowers in books. This is why the meeting was at the library; it was the place where the books were. Also, there were books that the members owned, and they brought these books with them when they came.

There were nineteen members of the botanical society. All of them were there. They were introduced to him one by one, all by name, and he shook hands with the men. With the women, he shook hands, but in a different way. He sort of held the ends of their fingers briefly. That was shaking hands with women. Then, they all sat down and began to talk. Someone had pots of coffee, and they drank from paper cups. The people of the botanical society were very concerned about him and Emma. Concerned, in that they felt he and Emma concerned them. That two botanists, or a botanist and an assistant, should be in the town was wonderful and quite reasonable. It was a fine town. Why shouldn't it have a botanist? Indeed, it had a botanical society. There was an immediate motion for Emma to give a talk about botany, which Emma refused to do for the time being. My work disallows it, she said.

THE CLAIMANT found that he was having difficulties again noticing when it was that someone was speaking to him. He found that he was having difficulty controlling his breathing, and he found that he was scowling or changing his expression when he didn't mean to do so. All of these things had been problems in the past, but now they had suddenly become meaningful to him. He had to fix these things if he was to become better for Hilda—if he was to be a person that Hilda would want to see and know. If she learned of the way that he was, well, she knew already. But, if it was confirmed to her that this was all that he could be, then . . . it didn't bear thinking about.

So, the claimant poured himself into his effort to be social, and he tried desperately to notice when he was spoken to, and to speak back regarding the subject. He asked questions when he didn't understand things, and he smiled as much as he could.

When they walked home, they would go under a street lamp, and the examiner would say,

—How careful you were back there.

and they would go out into the darkness past the light, and she would say,

—and how reckless!

—How careful . . .

—and how reckless!

—How careful . . .

—and how reckless!

It was a bit of a joke with her, for she had told him that this was the way that good learning proceeds. One must be careful at all careful points, and reckless at all reckless points. Those who are careful always get nowhere. Those who are reckless plummet.

When they got to the porch, she turned to him.

—What do you think about lying?

—I don't lie, he said. You know that.

—Aren't we lying about being botanists? asked the examiner. Isn't that a sort of lie?

—But, we spend all day drawing plants.

—Is there a time, she asked, when it is worthwhile for everyone—for you to lie, and then is it a bad lie? Or should all lies be found out, exposed, and the liars excoriated?

—Don't answer, she said. Just think on it.

And then she smiled at him. It was a warm, gentle smile. Such a smile she had never given him in all the time he had known her. With the flush of his success at the botanical society, he was off balance, and this smile swept over him. He suddenly felt that he should tell the examiner everything, that he should explain how he had met Hilda, and how she was plotting something, he didn't know what. He felt that he should lay the whole matter before her and do just what she said he should do.

After all, she had always done right by him. The things that Hilda had said about her examiners—that isn't how it had been with him.

And while he was thinking all this, the examiner went up the stairs, and he neither followed her nor spoke.

HILDA!

He thought he had spoken, but he had not.

The door was open before him. He was standing in her doorway, 23 Juniper Lane. She stood in the hall, in work garments, gardening clothes, rubber boots, a filthy shirt rolled up to the elbows, short trousers, and a thick cloth belt.

—I was just working in the garden. You are an hour early!

She came into the doorway and took his hand, pulling him into the house.

—Inside! Inside, quick.

—I'm sorry, he said.

—Don't be sorry, you fool. Close the door behind you.

She drew him up the stairs, past all the photographs and over the creaking boards.

—I LOVE YOU, he said.

—You fool, you fool, you fool, she whispered. Let us never talk of
such things. If it is true that there is only for me in this horrible
place one thing and that thing is you, and there is only for you
in this horrible place one thing, and that thing is me, then we
need not talk of love. Love is a comparison. I like him but I love
another. We are at the bottom of a ditch and there is just a parcel
of air to be found, a parcel and when it is done, we push at the
space, and another little space of air presents itself. Who can talk
of love? There is only air—or none, and if there is none then
there is nothing at all.

She spoke like this, on and on, forever chiding him when he
said this or that. I don't know how long I have been in these
places, really, she confided, it could have been forever. Have you
known anyone else, in all this time, he asked her. I have only
had the courage now, after all this time, to explain myself to
someone. And why me. Because, she said, because—you were
so dazed when I met you. You were still drifting inside. It was
the first time I could tell for sure that someone was a living
person, and not a shell like the rest of them.

—There are hundreds, maybe thousands of them, she said.
Thousands of villages. There is a world beyond it, I am sure
of that. But what the relationship is between the world and
the villages, I can't say. It seems that it could be that the world
created the villages, that the government over all, the republic,
made the Process of Villages in order to fix the people who
were ill, who couldn't bear the way the world was. It could also,
however, be the case that the government merely found the
villages, a separate society on its edge, and nurtured it. The
distinction is that the villages might be a part of the republic, a
subset of it—or they might be a separate thing, which are being
used by the republic to heal itself. If the sick people are placed
into the villages as part of an agreement between the villages
and the republic, then they are merely servants of the republic.
Then the examiners are bureaucrats of a kind, and the whole
Process of Villages is a massive bureaucracy.

—But, if the Process of Villages is just a place that grew up in a sort of passive antagonism to the republic, then it could be that sick people are abandoned there by the republic, and that the examiners are just the kind people who receive them, who receive them and nurse them back to health.

—Even where that abandoning takes place—should it take place at all, is in dispute. It could be that the fogging is a thing, a kind thing done by the Process of Villages, a gentle response to the horrors of the republic. Or, it could be that the fogging is what the republic does when it washes its hands of someone, and that it is something the Process of Villages has learned to deal with— almost as though it were a peculiar malady in its own right.

—But what is fogging?

—It is an injection. I figured out how to unlock the examiner's desk two houses ago, and I read the text they keep. The injection changes you, sends you deeper into yourself, in order that you can learn to protect yourself from life's difficulties. It does other things, too. It ruins your memory, and you lose most things you knew. That's why they have to teach you everything all over again.

—So, said the claimant. I was injected with something. That's what they did. They told me I was very sick, and that . . .

—You were very sick, and that you almost died. That you were on the edge of death, and you were rescued, and that now you are recuperating, yes, that is what they say. It is in the book, written down for them to say it. All the questions you will ask are there, and all the answers they will give. But, what we do not know, she said, is whether the book is true. It is possible that the book is a conditional lie. It could be all the truth that enables the examiners to do their job, with all the space around filled in with lies. In fact, it is quite likely that it is that. A thinking person could conclude nothing else.

The claimant felt that he was voyaging through a place of trees. The trees were rushing by, running like dancers in a long line. They danced around him, rushing and running and leaping. Their leaves fell across his face and their limbs tore at his clothing. He felt that he was falling and that the race of the trees kept him afoot. Each time he nearly fell, he was buffeted up and all the while, a great wind swirled in the distance. He wasn't going anywhere—he could not go anywhere—it was impossible, wherever one went, one would be rushed off one's feet, and held afloat in a mireless confusion.

As this feeling rose in him, she noticed that his face was changing, and she slowed her speech.

—Darling, she said, darling. It is all right. It is all right. We will find some way forward. I know we will.

—But what, he said, what could such a thing be? It is all hopeless.

And as he said it, he felt that it was true.

But then Hilda took him and kissed him and held him to her, and it was the strangest thing: he was sure suddenly that it was not the bedroom of Hilda's house that he was in, but that he was in another bedroom, in a house just like it, but one that he had never been in. And in Hilda's place, he saw another young woman, a person he had never seen in his life, but for whom he felt great respect, in whom he had great comfort, but who could it have been, who? and he was pulling her to him, and sobbing, and he felt her body all against his. His hands were in her hair, her soft yellow hair, and he grew calm, everywhere, calm. And then he was back again, back again in the house with Hilda. She was pulling away and standing.

—COME AND SEE, Hilda was saying.

They went into the study and stood by the desk.

—The lock is just there, she said. It can be picked, and all the answers are inside. I only managed to find the book and read some of it. Then I was moved and I got a new examiner. Martin is much more watchful. He speaks like an idiot, but it is all an act. He is a monster. I am afraid of him. Not that he would hurt me, but that he knows everything that I know, and more.

—Hilda, what is your real name?

—In the last place, where I failed, it was Kat. In the town before that, it was Morna. I don't even care about names anymore. If you could tell me my original name, it would be, it would be . . .

—What?

—It would be dirt, that's all. Just dirt. Not even worth putting in one's mouth.

IT WAS SEVERAL DAYS before he met her again. This time it was in the wood beyond the lake, just at dawn, as if they each had gone out for a walk and happened upon one another. That would be all right, they thought. Even if someone saw, such a thing would be all right.

They sat in the wood, by a stream. There was a stand of birch trees. He leaned against one and they spoke about this and that.

Suddenly, to Hilda and Martin, it felt very good to talk about nothing at all. They sat and made completely banal statements about the morning and the day and each other's clothing (which was practically the same), and they were very happy.

This went on until Hilda began to sob uncontrollably.

Martin tried to console her. When she finally spoke, she said,

—I need for us to have a plan. Otherwise, I am afraid—I am afraid we will just go on like this, living here. I am afraid nothing will change.

—But, what is there to do?

—I think we can leave, said Hilda. I think that it is possible to leave. It's true that people come. People who were not here before come here now. Even if for us it isn't entirely clear—I believe that I was in several villages before this, but it might not be true. I might always have been here: despite that, it appears true that others who were not here are suddenly here one day. If that's so, they come from somewhere, and we can go there, to the place where they came from, and to places beyond that. I'm sure of it.

Martin nodded.

She began to touch his hair and face, and he sat quietly in these attentions for some time.

—I have a present for you, she said.

She handed him several sheets of paper. They had been torn out of a book.

—Read them later. Goodbye for now.

The claimant sat in the wood and looked at the pages. They were, they must be—from the examiner's book. There in neat lines of type he found a description of the gentlest village as though it did not yet exist. He found a description of the role of examiner and rules for how an examiner ought to be. He was partway through such an explanation when he reached the end of the torn-out section.

If she had torn this out of the book, it must happen that they would discover it. Why would she give it to him? Would he now be guilty of her deed?

But something in him spoke up, and that voice said:

You are a fool if you think she did this for any reason but one: she loves you and wants you to be sure of her.

And a thick warmth rose in his chest and face.

He looked up. No one was near him.

He put the pages in his pocket, and set out home.

THE CLAIMANT woke, and he looked at the ceiling. It was the same plaster ceiling it had always been. The shapes of leaves were evident, shadows from the branches that abutted the window. His eye traced them and found a path from one end of the room to the other. He sat up and found his feet.

All of a sudden, he thought, all of a sudden, nothing is enough for me.

It was as if there were moments of strength in which he could understand everything that Hilda said to him, and then moments in which he felt that it was not worthwhile to, or that it was too much—that too much was required from him to do so. He thought again of the way the examiner had said—you must listen to stories, not to understand, but merely to be human. For Hilda, was it enough for him to just listen, or did he need to understand?

When she was there, he felt the injustice of the whole thing, and he wanted to help her, he wanted to act. But here, in the comfortable house, with the examiner and their botanical work, with their quiet breakfasts and long walks, he felt a long light dim evenly, all along the horizon. He felt what was bright and new grow worn. He knew that the sterling fierce things were no concern of his. He need seek no conflicts, no unveilings.

He was at the head of the stairs. He found his way down them, and to the table, and he began to draw. The examiner came in and sat next to him. She said nothing. She did not look at him. But a good feeling was there in the claimant. He was recovering. It wasn't a lie. He had been sick. He was sure of it. And then a thought rose in him. Maybe Hilda was sick. Maybe Hilda was still sick, and she had just deceived everyone. Maybe she was deceiving him.

There! He had spoiled the drawing.

He pushed it to one side, laid out another sheet, and started over.

THE EXAMINER took him for a walk that evening.

As he closed the gate, she asked him what it meant for something to die.

—What I am asking is, what is the meaning of death? If you wonder why I am asking, it is because, like everything else that we do here, this question is an arrow aimed straight at your recovery, your renewal. A person who does not know what death is can never be a healthy person. Such a person can only stumble along awaiting some final confrontation wherein their ignorance is exposed. At such a time, that person will learn, or break. So that you do not need to go to such a confrontation alone, we will speak of it now. And so, I ask you, what is death?

He closed the gate.

Her old face peered up at him. She had bound her hair back in a braid, and she wore a heavy coat unsuitable for the season. She often wore more clothes than were necessary. Of a sudden all her frailties came to light. She was much closer to death than he. How old was the examiner?

—You are thinking about my age, she said. When I ask you about death, it is my death that comes to your mind. And it is rightful for that to be the case. Your empathy gives you that gift. You empathize with my life and with my death, and so you think, this old woman, she is soon to die, and as you imagine my death and my passing, you experience it to some degree. What is that like?

THE CLAIMANT thought of the examiner, who had always been so strong, faltering. He thought of the triviality of it—that some random place should be the site of her death. That she would lie on the ground, everything spinning about her, and breathe her last. And then he thought of the uselessness of her clothing, of all the things that had been cut to her size, of all the tools that had been shaped under her hand, of everything in her life that had been measured to her—how useless it would all suddenly become. And he thought of how the world would rush into the space where she had been, and occupy it with something else. He began almost to cry, and tears gathered in his eyes. He felt very much that he loved her. She was his family, the whole of it. He loved her.

The examiner saw this, and took his hand.

—Walk with me, she said.

They walked up the street to where a thin path ran between rocks up a hill. They followed that path and came to a wrought iron gate at the hilltop, where a fence barred their way. The examiner opened the gate and they went through.

A long, rolling yard lay before them, going off down the hill to a distant tree line. Somehow the claimant had never been here before. His eyes crossed the landscape again and again, as if looking for something. He knew what this was. He was sure of it.

—These stone markers, said the examiner, they are called gravestones.

—Gravestones, the claimant repeated.

—No one uses these anymore. But once they were common everywhere. They make a clear point, and a resounding one, and so they have become a part of the Process of Villages. We re-create this cemetery in every village. It is even there in the distance in the gentlest village, though perhaps your eye did not find it there.

—But what is it? What are these stones for?

—Let's walk between them.

So, they walked up and down the lines of gravestones, and the claimant read them, and soon saw what they were for. The examiner said nothing, but looked on with her steady, impassive face, and did not indicate whether she thought that it was a good thing, this idea: cemetery, or whether it was a foolish human development that we were better rid of.

The claimant felt in the stones a great yearning. He felt that it was reflected in his own being at that very moment. The manner in which he was torn—his confusion in Hilda, of Hilda, about Hilda, his sadness for the examiner, and for her death— he felt very clearly what it was to be human at all and how it was encapsulated in the stones themselves.

—They are the error—our human error, he said. It's what makes it worth living at all. But also, it is completely irrational. They have no reason in them.

—What do you mean?

—I mean, if someone is dead, then that person is gone. A gravestone does nothing to fix that. And if it makes a place that others can go to be near the body of the dead person—then how does that help anything? It just prolongs the grieving. Better to simply pass on along the road, thinking nothing of it. But,

He kicked at the grass with his foot.

—But, if life is just that, just being reasonable, then there is nothing in it—nothing worthwhile. So, the yearning that we have to keep dead things living—or to make unreasonable things reasonable. That is why a person should live.

—Is it a paradox? asked the examiner.

—I don't think it is. I think the whole thought makes sense together. Neither side is complete.

The examiner smiled. She took something out of her pocket, a notebook, and wrote in it for a minute.

—I will die, she said. There are those who care for me, and they may be sad. But my life has had its effect, and will continue to have its effect after I am gone. I don't ask for more than that.

—Do you like the cemetery? she asked.

—I don't know, he said.

and then,

—Very much, I think.

—There were other purposes that cemeteries had in past times, said the examiner. A wealthy family could buy enormous monuments and display their power in cemeteries. Also, the splendor and expense of a grand funeral could intimidate a community and help to preserve the veil of power that a particular dynasty might have. It's also true that in cultures where patriarchal or matriarchal structures were quite strong, the passing of power through a family was of special importance. In such a time and place, events like funerals and weddings take on special importance, as the family drama becomes a societal drama.

BUT, THE CLAIMANT was no longer listening. They walked and walked along the green grass, cut by someone, always being cut by someone—it appeared to have been cut just then, or some hours before, it must have been—and he thought of his own life suddenly in proportion to the day in which he was alive, that very day in which he was standing.

I am alive, he thought, and now I am capable of living.

He suddenly felt very strong. And with the rising of his strength he felt an energy in him, a direction. He wanted to see Hilda and learn more. He wanted to know what there was to do, or whether anything should be done. The desire he had had to tell the examiner everything was still present, in fact, magnified by his vision of her death, but for him it was contingent on Hilda and what she would do next. Such a turmoil! It rose in him and rose, and then there flooded through his eyes the calm of the cemetery, of the close of evening, of this quiet walk. All the turmoil vanished as though it had never been.

Perhaps it was the patience of the examiner wearing off on him, or perhaps it was something else, but he felt a great strength in his legs, like a swimmer does. Under the green boughs of the cemetery, he did not need to do anything. No action was needful there, nor could be.

BUT, BACK AT THE HOUSE, when supper was through, he felt a lightness infect him, and with it he became brittle. The energy of his desire overbore him and he fell prey to it. Hilda, Hilda. She rose again.

The hour was coming when they were to meet. He sat and watched the clock. I should be getting to my feet, he thought. I should be going out the door. But, he didn't. The waters swept back. Again, it was as though he was beneath the green boughs of the cemetery. He stayed sitting there, and after a while, the examiner brought some tea, and they sat and played cards. When they were through and she had won once, twice, three times, they went upstairs to bed.

NOW THEIR RENDEZVOUS had been broken. There had
been a plan for them to meet, and they had not. It was simple
but it was bewildering. If he had wanted to see her, he would
have seen her. But he hadn't. Yet now, the claimant was thrust
suddenly back into his desire to see her. Nonetheless, he had not
gone. What would she think? Hilda had no real reason to come
to his house, nor he to hers. What could be done?

Yet, I can go to her house—perhaps not to talk to her, but to
speak to Martin. If he has befriended me, I can speak to him.
Then, she will be there and something can be arranged.

And in thinking of Martin, and of that house, he thought
again—what is the condition of their life? A sort of jealousy was
faint in his body. If they are to act as though married, do they
do so in the house when no one is there? If that is their cover, is
it kept at all times? And he thought of her flickering, how she
flickered and flickered, and the way that she had clung to him,
and he stood up. There in the kitchen of the house, he stood up
as if to go right then to see.

But, of course, this was foolishness. She was not his—not that
way. If to be safe, she needed to act a certain way, it was natural.
It was only natural. There was nothing moral in it.

Yet, he was in the front hall, and he was telling the examiner
he would go for a walk, and he soon found himself on Juniper
Lane, knocking at the door of a certain house.

—HELLO THERE.

The claimant froze. This was a person he did not know. He leaned back and checked the address on the door. 23 Juniper Lane. It was correct.

—I'm looking for, Hilda and Martin. I believe they live here.

—Oh, there must be some mistake, said the man. Hold on.

—Colleen, he called. Colleen, come here.

A woman came out of the door to the left, and approached them.

—What's up, Tom?

—This young man, he seems to think someone else lives here. Some, what were their names?

—Hilda, said the claimant. Hilda and Martin. I am sure. I was just here last week.

The couple laughed.

—Completely understandable, said the man. These towns do that to you. I know, because it has happened to me a time or two. Play tricks on your mind. Anyway, we have been here for thirty-five years.

—and counting, said the woman.

—and, I'd know it if we hadn't been here last week. Why, last week we had a barbecue. Matter of fact, you could have come, if we'd known you then. What's your name?

—Martin.

—Like the man you're looking for? Well, isn't that something. Are you looking for your own house?

He grinned at the woman.

—If it's true, it's a good trick. You can't find your own house, so you go door-to-door asking. And is Hilda your wife?

—No, no! I'm really looking for them. But, it seems . . .

The claimant overcame his desire to go past them into the house and look deeper.

—I'm sorry, I . . .

—Oh, no trouble. No trouble at all. It's good to finally get to know you. Martin, eh. I'm Tom. Tom Bedford. That's Colleen in the back room. She isn't very social these days, sorry about that. But, let me tell you. Our daughter is coming to visit. She is about your age, I'd say. Perhaps you'd like to meet her. We'll send an invitation to your house. How'd that be?

He excused himself and made his way back home. They must have removed her in the night. Those people must have moved into the house this very day, he thought. How could it have happened so quickly? Unless he was confused about the days. It sometimes happened . . .

But why would they have taken her away? Martin must have discovered something. Or, could it be—could he himself have given her away? Could that be it?

PARTWAY THROUGH THE NIGHT he woke. At first he
thought someone was in the room with him, but there was no
one—just furniture carrying the obscene shapes of shadows. It
was very quiet. Everything had grown as quiet as it could. He
held his breath and listened. Silence, silence, silence, and then a
light rap. Then silence, and a rap at the window. He looked out.
Someone must be out there. His eyes scanned the yard, moving
slowly from one end to the other.

There! She was there—it was Hilda, throwing bits of earth.
She had seen him at the window. She was crouching there in
the yard, waiting. He looked down from above—the street, the
fence, the yard, the porch, Hilda. Hilda!

Be as quiet as possible, as quiet as possible, he told himself. He
eased out of bed, and went down the stairs. Out the back door
and into the yard.

Hilda rushed to him.

—I went to your house, he said, there was . . .

And at the same time, she said,

—They took me away, they took me away, darling. Oh. I waited
for you and waited for you, and you never came, and then I went
back to the house, and Martin was there, and he was angry—he
was so angry . . .

—Took you away? Who?

—I woke up in the back of some kind of closed truck. They were
moving the bed that I was in. I was lying there, and we were
stopped for some reason. I jumped out the back and hid, and the
truck drove on without me.

They stared at one another. Hilda was not even wearing proper
clothes—just a nightgown. It must be true—they must have
taken her while she slept.

—They'll come looking for you. When the driver gets where he's going. When was this?

—Last night. I walked all day, and then hid and waited to come here. Look at my feet.

Her feet were covered in cuts from walking barefoot. One was partially wrapped with a cloth. It must be true.

—How did you find your way? he asked.

—What do you mean?

—From the road where you got out of the truck. How did you know where you were?

—There isn't anything out there. Just a road. It's just a road. I went the opposite direction the truck was going. As you approach the town, the waste turns slowly green. There are trees and grass, and then the town begins. I can show you. I don't know if there's time.

A great confusion and tiredness settled over the claimant. He felt that he was dealing with the situation and understanding it, moving through the details with celerity and sharpness, and then he wasn't. A weight settled and confounded all the variables. Everything seemed the same. He could make no progress.

—I don't know, he said. I don't know what to . . .

—Help me hide, she said. Someone is coming.

—Martin, Martin.

A voice was calling from the house. It was the examiner. A panic rose in the claimant's heart. He didn't want to do anything wrong. Nothing at all.

—I . . .

Martin hesitated.

—My love, said Hilda, you must . . .

She was pulling at him desperately.

—Help me. They're all against me.

—Martin!

The examiner's voice came from within the house.

The hall light came on, and then the light on the back porch.

There was an overgrown bush along the fence. Hilda pushed into it, and hid just as the examiner came out the door.

—Martin, she said. Is everything all right?

THE CLAIMANT stood there in confusion. He could hear the slight breathing of Hilda where she hid. The examiner stood looking down at him from the porch, a scant twenty feet away. What was he doing in the yard? Why was he there at all? What could he say?

He had never lied to the examiner. He didn't want to. She was standing there on the porch with a quilt wrapped around her. Her face was full of concern for him. If anything, her appearance in the middle of the night was even more aged than usual. He felt a sympathy for her, a profound worry. Also, he was terrified that he would be found out, and that she would be displeased.

—Martin, are you all right? Shall we get help? Come inside. Come with me.

The weariness that he had been feeling grew in him. He walked to the house and went up the steps. There he was, standing beside her. He found himself whispering, speaking to the examiner. He found himself talking to her, telling her things. What was he saying? What had he said?

The examiner looked deeply into his eyes, squeezed his arm, and nodded.

—Come into the house, she said.

They sat at the dining room table and the examiner made tea for them. She toasted bread and brought it out on a plate and they sat there. When they had been sitting awhile, there was a scream from outside.

—They have found her, said the examiner quietly. Don't worry, she will be all right. She is young and strong. But she is very sick.

She said this especially quietly.

—Hilda is very sick, and needs our help, she repeated.

She was holding the papers he had given her, the sheets from the book. He didn't remember having given them to her, and then suddenly he knew that he had. It hurt him to think of it. He had handed the pages to the examiner. He had pointed out where Hilda was hiding. He started to cry.

—You were right to get help for Hilda, said the examiner. Don't grieve over it. It was reasonable. It was the right thing to do. Now, let's get some sleep. Would you like something to help you sleep?

—Yes, said the claimant, I would.

They went upstairs. She gave him some medicine to drink; he lay down in his bed and slept long into the morning, and it was the examiner who woke him, saying,

—It is almost noon! Time to get up, time to get up.

And already then, the episode with Hilda felt far away. Had he ever known her? Had he?

AND THIS WAS how it was for him. Mostly, he was never worried about it—he felt that it was something that had happened to someone else, and he was untouched. Yet, sometimes, as when one looks in a mirror, when one hasn't seen oneself in a long time, and one catches sight of this face, one's own in a mirror, and feels—recognition, sometimes he was moved to a great sadness and he would almost cry. His face would twist and he would hold his head in his hands and think to himself: what have I done, and he would feel that he had betrayed the one person who was his.

At such times, the examiner would watch him with concern. When it happened twice in one day, a week after the incident, she came to a resolve.

I believe, she thought to herself, we have stayed here too long.

THE EXAMINER was standing at the bottom of the stairs when the claimant went to come down in the morning.

—When you come down the stairs, she said, you will not go up them again, not in this house, so come down slowly and purposefully and with full intent.

—What's that? he said.

—We are moving to a new village. This business with Hilda. It was not your fault. But, it is a failure of sorts. I am taking your name from you. Worry not—you will have another. You are not Martin anymore. I am not Emma. Do not refer to me as such.

—I should get my . . .

—You don't need your things. What we need is already there, in the place to which we're going. This travel is different from the ones we have done before, do you know why?

—Because you are telling me about it?

—That's right. I am telling you about it, so that you will know. I trust you. I feel you should know things. It will be the same in some ways. We will sleep while we travel, so we won't see much of it, and when we wake up, we will be there. I wanted to prepare you, and to give you your new name before you left.

—My new name, what will it be?

The claimant walked down the stairs, slowly, deliberately. He arrived at the bottom and stood over the examiner.

—Are you ready to hear it?

—I am.

—Henry, she said. Henry Caul. That is your new name.

—Henry, he said. Henry Caul. Henry Caul.

—Henry Caul, she said. It is time for us to be going. Come and sit with me on the porch. My name is Dahlia Gasten.

—Dahlia Gasten, he said quietly.

They went out on the porch and sat.

—Have some of this, said Dahlia. It will make you sleep, and then we can go.

She handed him a little bottle and he took it and raised it to his mouth. Had he seen one like it before? The end of the bottle was very small and it felt odd on his lips. He drank from it, and soon fell asleep.

Then they were there, sitting on the porch. The examiner sat on one chair. He lay asleep in another. A strange noise came down the street of the town, and it was a truck. A truck came into view and stopped before the house. Two men came out of it and picked up the claimant, one by the arms and one by the feet. They carried him to a pallet in the truck's rear, and set him gently down. The truck drove off, and soon its roar was as if it had not been, for a church bell was tolling in the distance, and insects buzzed in the near yard, and as the examiner rocked in her chair there was a faint creaking from the boards of the porch. Somewhere in the house a clock was ticking, and the tick went like this, tick, tick, tarick, tick.

4

THE CLAIMANT was awake and sitting up in bed when the examiner entered the room.

—Do you remember my name? she asked.

—Dahlia, he said.

—That's right, Henry. That is my name. Let us look around the house and see what we can see.

So, they both went around the house and looked at things. He saw that it was just the same as the other house had been. He looked at the dining room and all the walls of the dining room, the kitchen and all the walls of the kitchen. He looked out the windows of the kitchen and saw that the garden was the same, the garden and the street beyond. He saw that the hall was the same, and the stair, the bedrooms were the same. The examiner took him into the study, a place where he had never really been welcome before, and she said,

—This is the study. In this village, you are welcome here as much as I am. You can use this room, too.

She went to the desk that had always been locked.

—Here, she said, the desk is unlocked.

She opened it. There was a book within the desk, and also sheets of paper.

—This is where I put reports that I write about you and about your progress. The book here is the book of the craft of examining. It explains things about how to examine and why. It is a book like any other. Do you know what that means?

Henry was silent.

—It means that some parts are right and some are not. Every examiner makes decisions and does things in ways that are not doctrinal. I, for instance, constantly disobey the book in certain ways. In other ways, it is important to follow along. That's partly because we are not in this alone. You and I are part of a thing that is larger than ourselves.

She took the book out of the desk and held it up.

—It is not a very large book, as you can see. If you want to read it, you can. I will leave it in the desk. You can also read any of the reports that I write that you find in there. But, remember, do not be angry if you find things written about yourself that are true. If you read someone else's correspondence, there is always a price. One can often learn things about oneself that one didn't expect. It's rarely a comfortable experience.

She went out of the room and down the stairs, leaving him there.

He went to the desk, and closed it. He opened it again, and then he closed it.

Then he sat in the chair and looked at the desk from the outside. Hilda rose in his mind and fell away, and he felt good.

—I am becoming Henry, really, he thought to himself. I am much closer to Henry than I ever was to Martin.

He said this out loud, for he liked the sound of the names in his mouth.

—WHAT THINGS are there in every village? the examiner asked.

—Houses, said the claimant. There are many houses, and all of them . . .

—All of them are the same, finished the examiner. What else is there?

—There are shops. There is a general shop, and a shop for clothing. There is a shop where you can sit and drink tea. There is the restaurant. Above those shops are rooms where the people who work in them live.

—That's right, said the examiner. And what about the gathering places?

—There is the library and the village hall. There is the band shell.

—Have all these things been the same in all the places we have been, in all the villages—or have they changed?

—I think, he said, I think they have been the same.

—Do you think they have been the same, because they are the same, asked the examiner, or because you want them to be the same—because you are not differentiating between them? We could call that a case of their being—the same to you. Is that possible?

—I think, he said, I think they have been the same.

—But if they were different, she asked, would you have known?

—I think I would know, he said.

—And would it matter?

—I don't know. I don't think so.

—If it wouldn't matter, then isn't it a bit difficult to say for sure which way it was?

—I guess so, said the claimant. The villages are the villages—they are a place where we live. When I go in a direction, I know what I will find. When I return, I know it, too. The house is like that, also.

—What if you went to a place, asked the examiner, where things were not like this? Where everything was new?

—Things are always new. Even here. Isn't that true?

The examiner took out her book and wrote something down.

—LET US MAKE a new cover for ourselves. A new cover and what shall it be?

—I don't know, said Henry. I am having difficulty again, getting around. Maybe something where I don't have to move as much.

—Has it been disheartening for you? To not move well?

Henry nodded.

—You should have mentioned it to me. It will pass, said the examiner. It's just the medicine that helped you to travel. Perhaps you drank a bit too much. Too much can confuse the mind and the body. It will go away in a few days. Let's see now, your cover. Your costume for this town. What could your cover be? What about if you are working on a paper. I am the person who travels with you, not a servant, but a person who sees to your needs. You employ me that way. And you are working on an important paper for an upcoming conference. You are that age that you could be a scholar of some sort.

—A scholar.

—You don't need to talk about the subject. The less you do, the more interested people will be. The more you do, the less people will care, until if you were to talk about it all the time—they would actually avoid you. This is how such things are.

—But then, said Henry, what will we do? I won't actually be working on a paper. I don't believe I could do that.

—It is not the sort of thing you need to do. We will find other things to fill the time. We are working steadily toward our goal. Here is what we will do. Each day we will address our tasks. I will write my nightly report about it, and you can read it. Then you will know how you are doing. You will know how you are proceeding toward our goal.

—I will tell you, she continued, that a person like you, a good, solid person who knows what to do and when, can live where he

likes. We can find good work for you, and a place to live. You will
soon have all the skills of a normal human being, and you will
have the scope of a normal human being. You can even decide
whether you want to live in the villages, or whether you would
like to leave. Either is fine. I, for instance, would be perfectly
proud of you whatever you chose.

The claimant felt something wide and empty, like anticipation,
but weakened. It was not false, but it did not sound out like a
bell.

—For now, let's think about the things that you do well and the
things you like to do. We'll practice your interactions and we'll
talk about what frustrates you and what you fear. I have many
new exercises for you, and when we have gone through them,
we will be at the next step. Are you ready to begin? Remember,
too, Henry. You can fail again and again as much as you like.
What is the way to proceed?

—Desperately and cautiously, he said. First cautiously, then
desperately.

THE CLAIMANT was sitting in the study. These days he often liked to come there. He would sit in the study and move things around on the desk. The book was there, and the reports. He could read them, finally. He hadn't even really known they were there, but now he knew and he could read them.

The truth was, though, that he did not read them. He had no desire to. Somehow, that they were available to him was enough. If they said one thing or another—he was sure it would be just about the same. There was a voice in him that rebelled at this, a voice that shrieked, screaming to him over broad distances to pore over the book, to read the reports, to glean everything that he could. But since Hilda had gone, that voice had grown weak, and he could scarcely hear it.

Now, he rode high on all the praise that he was receiving. Daily, he was moving forward with his good nature and he found that he could speak to people and accomplish things in the world in the most startling ways.

The examiner would say to him something like,

Tomorrow, you are to go to the restaurant in the town. The restaurant will be full of people. It will appear that there are no more tables. The situation will be: you cannot eat at the restaurant, as there is nowhere to sit. A young man will be there also, waiting. You will hear him being told, you cannot eat here now, as the restaurant is full.

But, you will approach the host and you will ask if there is a table, and the host will smile and incline his head. He will shout something over his shoulder and a table will be brought out and set up. The young man will be watching you and wondering who you are that such a thing could happen, and you will invite him to sit and eat with you as if it is the most natural thing in the world.

Then you will sit, and he will ask you many questions about your life, none of which you will be able to answer. The reason is this: you do not remember the events of your life. Such is your plight. But, you will not lie. You will merely explain that you were ill but you are grown better, and that you are working now on a paper to present.

When the young man leaves, he will invite you to meet him again, but you will decline, and if he asks why, you will say that you are very busy. You will feel a flush from the wine that you have had, and it will be difficult to decline this invitation, as the young man is very charming and his company is a great pleasure, but you will do so.

Why will you do it? You will do it because it is a part of life also that you must train for—to have a strong will, and to be able to turn down good things. That is the exercise for tomorrow.

And then it would happen that on the following day, Henry would go down to a restaurant, and he would do so not because he remembered to, but because he was hungry, and he had begun to eat at the restaurant sometimes. And at the restaurant, when arriving, he would notice that the tables were all full, and he would feel a vague worry that he could not be sat at a table. And as he approached the host, he would notice a young man being turned away. And the host would notice him standing there, would notice Henry, and the host would say, Henry Caul, our distinguished guest. Henry Caul, Henry Caul. The name would burnish and shine with a sort of proud energy. Then Henry would be shown to a table that had not been there a minute before. The table would actually be carried over the heads of many other guests, and tables would be pushed aside to accommodate it. Candles and the like, fancy silver, fine porcelain all would be placed upon the table, and the whole matter would unfold like a fan. And while this was happening and everyone was standing mesmerized watching it, Henry would say to the young man, your name, sir, and the young man would say, my name is Sasha, and Henry would say, come and sit with me, why not. Then the two would sit and they would not even need to order. The waiters would attend them who do not need to be told what is wanted; they merely bring what is best, and take away any number of unwanted things without rancor. And Henry would speak with Sasha, and Sasha would ask questions, he would say, Henry, if you don't mind my asking, where are you from? What is that accent? And Henry would say, I do not know. That is the type of fact with which I am unacquainted, and the reason is this: I remember very little of the past. You see, I have been convalescing and am just now returning to life. At the moment, I am working on a paper for an upcoming conference.

Then, Sasha would ask about the paper, and Henry would say, I am not in the business of talking about papers that are not complete.

And someone would come to the table with a letter and present it to Henry, saying, Professor Caul, here is a letter for you, just arrived. And Henry would put it into a pocket in his coat. He would not even look at it.

When the dinner was through and they were standing before the restaurant, when the lights of the restaurant were practically turned off, and Henry had heard all about Sasha's childhood, his current work, his fascination with sandpipers, they would bid each other goodbye, and Sasha would ask to meet again and be denied, and this denial would touch Henry less than he had thought it would, for he would be prepared, completely prepared for this, just as he was now becoming completely prepared for all things. Then he would walk home along the avenues, and the examiner would be waiting for him on the porch and she would clap her hands twice and smile, and he would smile back.

Or the examiner would say, tomorrow you will be walking down the street. A man will trip and fall and his knee will be injured. He will be bleeding just a little. You will be carrying your jacket over one arm, and you will use it to staunch his bleeding. It will not be a serious wound. All the same, you will staunch it, and help the man up. You will give him your arm and accompany him to his house, and when he invites you in, you will join him for a glass of wine. When his wife gets home, they will ask you to stay for dinner. They will insist upon it, but you will say that you have work to do. In this case, you will demur even from saying your name. You will say this sentence, for the time being I would like to be an unnamed guest, and if you do it right, they will respect your wishes.

And then, it would happen that Henry would go out walking and he would be passing along a crooked avenue where the pavement was a bit uncertain, and there he would witness a man falling to the ground. The man's pant leg would be cut open and the skin of his leg would be broken, and there would be blood there, on the leg and on the ground. Without a second thought, Henry would wrap the leg and apply a good deal of pressure. He would speak in a gentle voice to the man, and he would lift the man to his feet—but only when the man was ready. At the man's house, he would share a bottle of wine, and when asked about himself, he would obfuscate, and his obfuscation would be kindly met, for it would have been laid out in the gentlest and kindest way. Also, the supper would be avoided with the same light stratagem, and away Henry would go, across the village and back to his house.

It never occurred to him to wonder how there could be so many people, so many shifting groups that he only saw once in so small a village. No matter how many such scenes played out, he didn't wonder—for Henry had become a very particular sort of person. He had been groomed to be a person who did not ask questions. He had not been told to be that way, but all the same he had been led to it, and now that he was there, he felt a great comfort.

Yes, those are the sorts of things that would happen. Not those things, exactly, of course, but things like them. Many things just like them.

—HOW IS IT that you know when you have accomplished
a conversation with another person in a good manner? asked
the examiner slowly. Or, I should say, how do you think other
people judge these conversations?

They were eating supper, pea soup with thick, crusty
brown bread. The claimant had a piece of bread torn in half
on his plate. The brown bread tore well and it felt good to
do it.

—I think it is a success if we can both go away feeling that
we were right to begin with. That we were right about how
it would go when we met and talked, and that it went the
way it was supposed to go.

—Who determines how it is supposed to go?

—No one does. But, if it doesn't go that way, everyone can
see it.

—And would that embarrass you?

—No, I don't think so.

The claimant thought for a minute.

—I don't think about other people judging it.

—Why?

—Because, you said, you said once, that it is a failure to
think of people as being separate from the village. The
people are the village. If I speak to them about something,
I'm just trying to preserve the sense that already exists in
the village. I do that by having a sensible conversation, such
a conversation as could happen in the village. That is
the whole of it.

The examiner clapped her hands together.

—One more thing, she asked. I want to do an exercise. I want you to tell me what it is like to walk down into the town. Could you do that for me? Imagine the most beautiful day imaginable, a day such as you have longed for. You wake up, and go downstairs. You leave the house. You go out into the street. Take it from there.

—I GO OUT into the street, said the claimant. The gate shuts behind me. I'm surrounded by houses that I know, good houses, all the right dimensions, all painted the way that I like. The road goes by, and I go along it, I find the fence and I walk beside the fence. We are on a hill and at the bottom of the hill, there are other sorts of buildings. I think about the things that I will see, and then I see them. There are shops, and people in the shops. Often the same people are in the shops, the same people buying things, the same people selling things, the same things being bought and sold. There is a shop where clothes are mended, a cafe where an old man sits by himself in front of a chessboard, and another old man is sitting down to join him. He doesn't sit down. He stands there next to it. They both look at the board. There are benches farther on, and the people who sit in the benches vary by the hour. When I am there, it is usually early or it is late. When it is early, there are people there who I know, people I recognize from one set of places. When it is late, there are people I recognize from another set of places. The people go elsewhere and are replaced. Then, we come to a little square, and . . .

—Very good, said the examiner. That is enough for now. Let's finish our supper.

She raised her glass.

—This is how people toast, she said.

THEN, A DAY CAME when the examiner was not there. He looked about the house for her, but he could not find her. On the kitchen table, there was a note. The note said:

✚ ✚

Gone for two days. You will be perfectly all right until I return.

✚ ✚

Henry fell into a small confusion, but passed over it lightly. It should be no concern for her to go away. He was prepared for that. In fact, he spent most of his days now on solitary tasks. There was food in the house, and if he wanted to, he could go out to eat. If he wanted company, he could find it outside. He could visit the home of one of his acquaintances, for instance.

At that thought, though, he did become concerned. He was not sure which of them he would go to, and what it would mean to do so. He had better not go visiting.

Although, he supposed, it didn't much matter whether it was one or another home that he visited. He could imagine what the visits would consist of, and it wasn't like anything at all would come of them. He didn't need to be afraid of consequences. Whatever he chose would be fine. Even if the examiner were here, he might not tell her where he was going. So, why should it matter?

Slowly, slowly, in this new place, a measure was taking its course. He was stiffening into a new resolve—a stolid manner was gripping him. He was not blunted so much as immobile.

Many things will be said to me, and I will say many things. Such was his thought in the morning, and in the night he might think, many things were said to me, and I said many things. But what those things were—they were unreachable. They were like mouths yawning open a brief second and then closing, yawning in succession.

If he had once thought life was different from this—then he no longer suspected it might ever have been the case.

AND THE NEXT TIME she went away, it was for a week, and then, every so often, she would simply be gone with no notice, and he became comfortable even with that.

It came to pass that the exercises the examiner presented him with ceased to be rehearsed. She would not tell him ahead of time how they would go. He would simply travel out into the village and things would happen and he would respond. Sometimes things would go well, and sometimes they would go badly, but either way, it was always all right. He would talk about how they had gone with the examiner. Or sometimes, he would not. Sometimes it was okay for things merely to have happened. As the examiner said, events are just events. Nothing is any more important than anything else.

Once, he got into a heated argument with a loud woman who had knocked him with her umbrella. By the end of the argument, though, his good nature had won through, and they were both apologizing. They were standing in the rain, both drenched now, and apologizing for their behavior.

Once, he left his coat on a bench and the next day he saw someone else wearing it!

Once, he was asked to give a speech at a small gathering, and when he arrived—they had forgotten he had been invited at all.

These and other things he learned he could bear. His nature became seamless with that of the village. Others began to comment on it—what an example he now was setting. They said these things just loud enough for him to hear.

THE EXAMINER was sitting in a room that was in the house, but that the claimant had never seen. It was on the other side of a wall, and he had never thought to look at the house from the outside to see that the windows matched up with the rooms. She was sitting at a desk, like the desk in the study, and she was writing something down in a report. This is what she wrote:

✚ ✚

Claimant has reached his ease. Claimant is at ease, and there is little more to do. I believe that he was once an extraordinary candidate and must have been extremely high functioning when he came to us. My guess is that several years have passed since then. The person that came into my care has never had any potential for a real existence. He is now capable of a mediated and comfortable life, albeit with no responsibilities, and with constant maintenance. I recommend that he receive no real duties at all.

Although it is not knowable, as per the regulations of the process, I estimate that the claimant has been reprocessed a minimum of eight times. If true, that is lamentable, and is well beyond what I believe should be permitted.

As for the claimant, it is necessary he be under constant supervision. For that task, I recommend examiner 2387. She is connected with the case already, and can be reintegrated without trouble. Indeed, there is every reason to think he will look forward to her company.

At or before the year's end, then, I will conclude this case, and leave village E6.

I look forward to the group analysis of this case.

✚ ✚

TIME PASSED. After some number of days, one particular day arrived, and in the midst of that day, it was midday. The sun was shining so brightly overhead it seemed that every blade of grass could be made out, each from the others. It was a sort of harmony—nothing could be hidden, nothing at all beneath the sky.

Up and down the streets of the village, people went, and where they went it was about their meager business. There was just enough business for them to do. Just enough, and they were glad. The water flowed in the streams. The water stood still in the lake.

Here and there, a person would pause, and meet the eye of another person. There would be recognition and a glimmer of pleasure. Here and there, a person would enter a house, and shut the door, and the door would shut well. It would close with a dark and solid sound.

Likewise, windows were being thrown open. Other windows were closing. Here and there, a person was lying down for a nap, or pulling out a chair to sit at a table. The village was full of objects and things and they were all in use. It was a merry contraption, an intricate and many-faceted thing. From its center to its edges, it was complete in itself. If there were things it did not admit, and there must always be, then there is no room to speak of them now.

THE EXAMINER set a brass plate on the gate at the front of the house. On it was the name Henry Caul. Come and have a look, she told him.

She called him down out of the house, and he came hurrying, just as always. As always, he did, and when he did, they stood there and something marvelous happened. He was standing there and thinking about the brass plate. He was thinking about the name Henry Caul. He was thinking about the gate and the house and the street. And the examiner said out loud, out loud she said to him—

—Henry Caul is now your real name. Go for a walk and return to the house, and see how your name is here on this brass plate.

Then Henry went down the street, and every house that he passed had a person in the yard, and every person called out to him, good evening, Henry, or Mr. Caul, how nice to see you. He knew them all, every one. He knew them, and they knew him.

He went down one street and another. He looped back, and all the glimmering, shining faces fluttered together, all saying, Henry, Henry, Henry.

AND AS HE WALKED up the front steps of the house, he heard voices. Voices within his house! Two people were talking. The examiner was in the dining room with someone. Who could it be?

The examiner, his good friend, Dahlia, the person he had known and lived with for so long, she who had just put out the brass plate with his name, she who was so pleased with him, she came out into the hall and took his arm, and led him, not into the dining room, but into the parlor. They sat. He looked back in the direction of the dining room, but the examiner caught his eye and held it.

—I know that it has been difficult for you, Henry, to deal with the failure that happened last year, that happened in the last village. Indeed, it was not a failure. You did very well, but it was a failure of the village. Things with the woman called Hilda did not go well. She was very ill, and it hurt you to have to do the right thing. It hurt you because she was so persuasive, and because you were still vulnerable to her way of thinking. You are a loyal and good person, and you wanted it to be true that there was another kind of help you could have given her, but in the end your instincts won out and you found that there was only the one sort of help. You gave her that one sort of help. Yet even now you think about it and it troubles you. The world is a difficult place. It puts us in difficult situations. And now you have learned how to deal with all of these situations.

The examiner took a deep breath.

—I want to introduce you to someone, she said. This person has come to see us. She has come to live in this village for a while. Her name is Nancy. Nancy Throtten. You will see, see that there is a reason she came here.

—Nancy, said the examiner. Nancy, come in.

She leaned in, and whispered in the claimant's ear.

—She remembers nothing about what happened, so don't confuse her by talking about it. I think she will remember you a little, though, perhaps a little at first. So, be kind. If I remember right, you enjoyed spending time with her. Perhaps you will again?

There were footsteps in the hall, and then,

The young woman who came into the room was wearing a lovely periwinkle dress with thin straps, and bright yellow stockings. She was very pretty, so he thought, and when she saw him, she turned her head slightly to the left and smiled.

It was Hilda. Hilda!

—Dahlia has been telling me all about you, said Hilda-Nancy. I am looking forward to getting to know you.

The examiner left the room and the two young people sat together on a small couch.

—I feel, said Hilda-Nancy. I feel almost as though I had known you for a very long while. But, that's silly.

She laughed, a bright wistful laugh.

—I have only just met you. We have all of that before us. Henry, she said. Henry, it is such a good name. I do love names. Don't you?

—Nancy is a good name, too, said Henry. I think it fits you very well.

And as he stared at her, he felt in himself the past receding. He remembered, as clear as day, that he had lived in another place, and that he had known someone named Hilda, but that and other things like it seemed not to matter at all. Here was Nancy, here he lived in a place where certain things were. They were. That was enough. There was no need to think back to other things, or to let them rise up in the mind. His face assumed a studied posture—from without he appeared to be a person thinking deeply, but in fact, he was merely sitting there, calmly waiting for something to happen. Nancy's face bore the same beatific expression. They were holding hands, and anyone who looked into the room would suppose that they were the two happiest people in the world.

On the other side of the wall, the examiner stood quietly, her eyes shut. She clapped her hands once, and then again, but so softly that no one could hear.

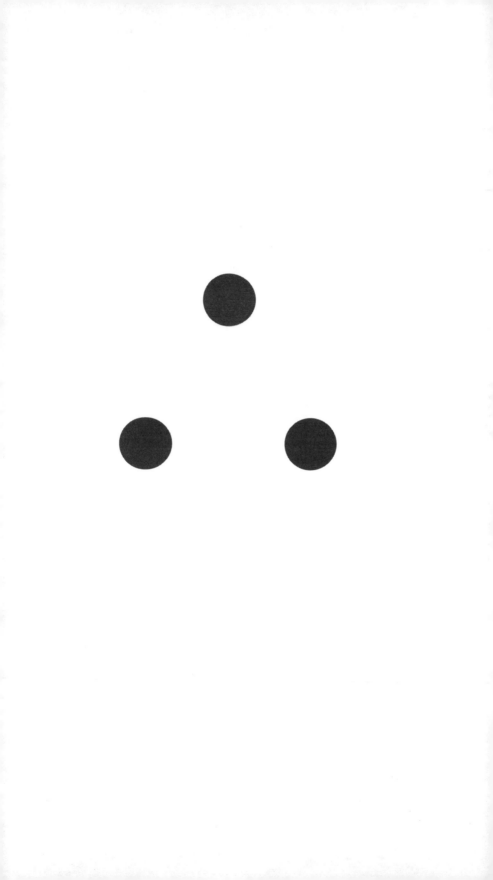

[
A
PLACE
YOU
GO
LAST
]

IT WAS A MAZE of hallways, a plain building with a maze of hallways. Most of the offices were empty. The doors were unmarked. No one waited before them.

Yet, on one door, there was printed a simple title. It was simple, but puzzling. It read:

INTERLOCUTOR

In the hall opposite, there was a bench. A man, a petitioner, had been sitting on the bench for the better part of an hour. His face and clothing were worn and thin and lined as though he hadn't slept. His hand was shaking, and he was holding it in his other hand. Perhaps both were shaking. He stared mutely at the floor, and the light over his head flickered fitfully.

Finally, the door opened. A man with lustrous white hair, an old man, wearing a black suit, was looking out. He inclined his arm, and the petitioner stood, walked into the room, and shut the door.

As I sat in the office of the cure, he began to speak and explain to me what it was. I was there, and I had no choice but to continue, it seemed there was nothing but that, nothing else—and yet, it was being explained to me, almost without my permission, as a matter of course, this thing I did not understand: the cure for suicide. There had been so much progress in the world at large. So many things were solved, so said the interlocutor. My grand-father and his grandfather, even more so the grandfathers of those grandfathers, they could expect much less than I can, and so on and so on: the general life of man is improving at breakneck speed. But, the solutions all have had consequences, and the worst of these, it crops up again and again, he said, is isolation. In the modern world, we, all of us, are isolated. We might as well be furniture, he continued. That is, we cannot feel—we cannot reach out to others; again and again the problem comes up. *There are those who cannot continue.* Therefore, now that so many problems had been solved, this was the feeling in the republic, it fell to us to confront this final problem, this problem of problems. It fell to us to find a solution, a cure for suicide, so said the interlocutor. His white hair was feathery and avian, but comforting, and seemed to declare that he was fit for the position he held, whatever position it was. Interlocutor. What was that? He had the same chair on both sides of his desk. The desk was basically a table. He could have sat on either side and it would be the same. I was here to speak to him and he to me. So he said. He said, the Process of Villages was created out of nothing. There was no such idea anywhere, and then suddenly it was a success. Suddenly, depart-ments like this one were created in every city. This department was only a month old. He explained things rapidly, unendingly, and then suddenly would lapse into silence, watching me for unaccountable reasons. He said, the interlocutor, he himself, had just arrived in the city a week before, but he had worked in a different office, an office of the so-called Department of Failure, for many years. That's what they call it, the Department of Failure,

so he said. Regular folk. The real name is just its function: Process of Villages. It is the way the cure is administered. This is the beginning. When he said that, he made
a curious gesture of his hand, as if to diminish the whole
thing—to make it seem possible. A beginning is easy, so
he seemed to say, and from there, it is all taken care of. I
felt that he looked a bit like my grandfather, a man I had
never liked. But, in him, all the elements of my grandfather that were deplorable and wicked were somehow
lightened and improved. It was as though this thing,
grandfather, had been revisited with greater care in his
person, and now here he was, interlocutor, a person with
whom one could speak. He said, for a very long time, for
a thousand years and a thousand years before that, it was
thought that suicide was wrong. It was believed that one
shouldn't kill oneself, that one didn't have that right. This
was because of a false idea—that the body was not one's
own property—that it belonged to someone other than
you. Whether that was God or some other man, the
reasoning was the same. But now we can see, there is no
reason, really, not to end your life if you no longer want to
live it. In fact, living it—provided you don't want to—is
irrational, so said the interlocutor. A man was sitting
where you sit, right there, not three days ago, so said the
interlocutor, and he said to me, I have never been the
person I want to be. Even as a child, I was someone else.
Every morning, for a lifetime—a lifetime!—I have woken
up in this body that I feel should not be my own in a
situation not my own. Why should I not end this life. My
reply to him, said the interlocutor, was, if the idea is that
you want out, why should it not be so, but consider this:
Groebden, Emmanuel Groebden—one of the finest minds
this world ever produced, he struggled with this problem.
It was as if he spoke with you, with you alone, and heard
your troubles, and solved them. His solution was this, the
Process of Villages, so I told him, said the interlocutor. So,
I said, not three days ago. I told him, we will allow you a
complete reinvention. You now have this choice, a choice
that men have never had—not in a hundred thousand

years of life—to start over completely. That is what we are
here for, and that is how we will help you. And, continued
the interlocutor, looking at me, we offer the same help to
you. Even now, that man who sat where you are sitting,
who sat there sobbing uncontrollably, he was wretched,
just wretched, sobbing in that chair—even now, he is
peaceful and partway on a new journey. He made a
sweeping gesture with his hand. There are, though, said
the interlocutor, many formalities to be addressed. That is
why I am here. We are to speak, you and I, and I am to
learn about you, to classify you, to see to you and find out
why it is that you are here. So said this man who was the
mirror image, the spitting image of my grandfather, a
man I had hated. I, too, was wretched, I thought. I,
wretched, was there, sitting in this office, and I was to tell
my wretched story. Very well. He was speaking anima-
tedly. This was a part of his repertoire that was well
rehearsed. He said, do you know how it will be in the
place you have just left? The place I have left? The place
you have left—the house you have left, the people you
have left, the body of their communications and thought,
their livelihoods, their esteems, their hopes—do you
know how it will be settled, your coming here? It is this
way: Everyone who has known you well will separately
receive a small envelope in the post. The envelope will be
opened, and when it is opened, there will be within it a
yellow slip. Whoever has opened it will find a yellow slip.
He or she will draw out the yellow slip and on it there is a
name written. Clement Mayer. Your name. They will read
this name to themselves. Some will say it out loud. When
they open this envelope what will happen is that they will
know that you are no longer in their lives, that this person
is gone forever and cannot be found or reclaimed anywhere in the world. This is a comfort for you. You may
know that all books will close, that all unfinished ends
will finish, neatly. There is no looking back because there
is no back. The tying off is complete, so said the interlocutor. I asked him if there was a time when a person had to
continue forward. I asked if at some point in the process,

one could not go back to the old life. Do you want to go
back to the old life? I do not want to, I said, I am here for
one reason, but I was thinking, for another individual,
perhaps, they are here and learn this information, and
then they stand up and leave the office, go back to the
street and find their way across the city to the place where
they live and the people they know. You can leave, right up
until the last, said the interlocutor. You could leave now.
I have no intention of leaving, I said. There is, though, he
said, a matter of proof. It is lamentable, but we have found
it necessary to require a proof of sorts. We like to hear
your account of yourself. We do this so that we can be
sure that you are in the right place—that you are, in fact,
reaching for the hand that we extend. He said this quickly,
twice, once to me, and then once to himself almost under
his breath. Reaching for the hand that we extend. A
woman was here, he said, the first person I dealt with in
this city, she had a large family and was a great success in
government. I believe you would know her face if I were to
show it to you. I looked out of my office, I opened the door
just as I opened it to admit you, and there she was. I
brought her in, sat her down, and at first she could give no
account of herself consonant with a need for our help.
Every facet of her life was flawless. She was a marvel, she
really was, a sort of titan of life's powers. But, we sat here
for a very long time. It became dark outside, and I felt—I
will wait. I don't need to go home. I have nothing especially to return to tonight. I can do this work some hours
more and there will be no harm. And as we sat, she began
to talk about other things, not just things from her life,
but things from other lives, other things that were a part
of her so-called mental life. And as we traveled deeper
into this thing—she said it was a sort of mental life, I
began to feel a certainty. This was a woman that wanted to
be parted from everything that she knew. She was not in
grief. She had no tears to cry, nothing to lament. But she
was finished. The duration of her interest in her life was
shorter than the duration of her life. She was in an
existential predicament. I said that to her and she did not

agree. She thought such a formulation was revolting. We did agree, however, so said the interlocutor, that the treatment was, for her, quite necessary. She filled out the appropriate contracts, and although it was then around eleven p.m., I made the necessary arrangements and she continued on. She did not need to go home again. She simply continued on, once I had made the arrangements. Or, continued the interlocutor, there was a boy, only sixteen years old, who had, as he put it, started out wrong. Everything about his beginning was the incorrect beginning. I met him not in this office but in the previous office. He was quite a fresh-faced darling, very sweet and straightforward, answering every question with his utmost effort. But all his youth was undercut by a dense black grief. He had been deeply misunderstood, right from the get-go. There was nothing for him. At first, I was sure I would dismiss him, send him back. I am sending people back all the time, all the time. But, when he laid out the situation, not as a child would, but as though he were a long veteran of the world, well, I had to capitulate. I gave him what he wanted, and I am sure that he is in good stead. The interlocutor was talking, but he was waiting. He was talking, but waiting for me to speak. His talking was a form of permission for me: this is a place for talking, his talking said. The idea that I would speak about my situation was unbearable to me. I said that, I said to him, the idea that I would speak about my situation is unbearable to me. When I learned about the Process of Villages, and that this department was the door to it, the entryway, so to speak, I felt, not hope, for I have none, but a wish that I could cross that threshold speechless, saying nothing. If it were that way, said the interlocutor. I know that I must speak about it, I said. I know that. Then the interlocutor moved his chair a little to the left, as if to prepare himself for something that was coming, and the thing that he was preparing himself for was that I was starting to speak, and what I said was this. Imagine that you are a young woman. Imagine your name is Rana, Rana Nousen. Imagine that you live in a house of great

wealth, that you have a fine education, friends, a delight-
ful family. But, that one day, you go to a doctor because
you have been having headaches, some pressure in your
head, and at the doctor's office you discover you will die. It
is certain. You will soon be dead. It could be drawn out, or
it could be swift: that much was uncertain. But that you
will die is completely incontrovertible. The doctor doesn't
even qualify a word. The verdict is complete. And you are
standing there, and everything, all your fine things turn
to ash. Just the same, they shine twice as brightly—every
good thing is possessed by the utmost fineness of its
nature, for it is suddenly finite—that which was infinite,
in a long life, suddenly finite. You leave the office, you go
down a street, down one street, down another. And on
that day, on that very worst day, you meet a young man.
For whatever reason, you think that he is quite wonderful
He, though he may have qualities that do not raise him up
above others of his kind, seems to you to be very remarkable, so I told the interlocutor. You, Rana, stand in the
street and speak to him. You are exchanging pleasantries
that become rapidly tinged with a meticulous seriousness.
In the course of a small conversation, the two of you find
that you want to keep seeing each other. And so, you see
to it that he has your address, and you go off. You go off
home, and at home you are surrounded by your family.
You tell your family the news: you are to die. Your best
friends are summoned to the house. They are told:
you are to die. Everyone is gathered there, and it is an
atmosphere of loss and sadness. Then, you address the
group and what you say is this: you say, there are three
months left to me. I want to have them. If they are mine,
and they are, then I don't want to speak about this illness
again. Everyone here must swear to never speak of it until
I am gone. I am going to leave the room and wash my face
and hands. When I come back in, in five minutes' time,
you will all be having a nice gathering that has nothing to
do with me. We'll have food brought in and we will have
an evening such as we might have had before the news of
today. And please, you add, do not be constantly at my

service. That isn't the life I have led, nor is it the life I want to lead. Then you leave the room, and when you return, your family and friends, so sophisticated and strong are they, that they hold to your wishes. A perfectly acceptable evening goes forward, and at some point in the night, the guests all go home, so I told the interlocutor. Now, the next day, there is a knock at the door of your house. It is the young man. His name is Clement. He wants to see you, and you find that you want to see him. Although he is rather poor and not at all remarkable, you find it in your heart to go on an outing with him. This outing brings you closer together. Soon, a week has passed and you have seen him every day. Your family and friends are astonished. You seem to have changed—and grown even more brilliant. You appear to glow—so happy you have become. When you sit about on bridges, kissing this young man, or when you lurk late into the night at motion picture stalls, or drinking counters, you feel that finally it is here—a life you have always wanted. Some-how, though you must have known other wonderful men, other boys, before this, Clement is to you a thing for which to be grateful. Although he does not, cannot understand this, he does not need to. To all his protesta-tions that he is beneath you, you laugh and laugh. You are always laughing at him and calling him to account for his faults and then laughing more, for to you they are noth-ing. As the situation continues, you see that some you know, your mother, your father, are growing concerned. You worry that they will tell him, that they will spoil everything. So, you tell them, so you tell your friends, say nothing to Clement of what you know. This I told the interlocutor, sitting in his office, my head in my hands. The room became quiet, was suddenly quiet, had been quiet for a long, long time.

I looked at the interlocutor and he was looking at me. I said, she and I, we met, and some months passed. Some

months passed, and I said to her, Rana, why don't we take
a car into the country. We are always here in the city with
other people around. Why don't we go somewhere where
people aren't. It might be nice. She was nervous about the
idea, so I told the interlocutor. I could see that. She
appeared to fear the idea that we would go into the
country. Despite the fact that this was a perfectly ordinary,
a perfectly acceptable idea, it nonetheless brought a
reaction that I could not in any way have anticipated. Away
from the city? She was unnerved. Her face became pale.
But, she was such a strong person, was always ahead of
me, always more consistent, more sharp, and so now that
I had hit upon this weakness, I leapt. I said, actually said,
I can hardly bear to say it now, but I said to her, I told the
interlocutor, I said, come now, you aren't afraid of going
into the country? She said she was not afraid of going into
the country. If I wanted to go, we would go. She said this
simply, and somewhat breathlessly. I was pleased. Then,
why don't we do it? I continued ruthlessly. It doesn't
matter to be where we can be with other people, where
there are services, things, rooms full of belongings, does
it? No, she said, it doesn't. But, I could see that she *was*
afraid, and I could not see why. Still, I pushed her. And so,
one morning, when no one was around, we loaded up her
car with some canvas bags and a suitcase, and drove out of
the city, to spend a week at a house her parents had. They
had many houses, and this one was nearby—it was in the
country, two days' drive away. To that house, we drove.
She cried a bit as we left, and I couldn't see why. She was
crying and I tried to console her, I said, Rana, what is it?
And she would only say, nothing, nothing, nothing.
Nothing, nothing. When I pressed her, she said that she
didn't know. It had come over her, she didn't know why.
What it was she was feeling, she deemed, was unexplain-
able. I did not press her. I said something like, well, I am
sure you will feel better once we are in the country. That is
probably true, she agreed. As we drove, she sat sometimes
in the seat beside me, the passenger seat, and when she
did she would sit turned so that she could watch me.
The top of the car was down, and so her hair would be

blowing away in the wind, or alternately she would bind it back with a cloth, and then it would go nowhere, it would just sit neatly beneath the cloth as the wind beset her face. Either, in the first situation, she would allow her hair to be loose, and she then would appear to me out of the corner of my eye as some blinding valkyrie, some effulgent flood of a thing, beauty knowing no boundaries, burning at the edges of itself, or she would bind it down, bind her hair down in a simple cloth, and in binding it down she would transform, all this in the corner of my eye, into a perfect outline of a thing, a nature of natures, a sylph or naiad. This was my passion. I would look at her, actually turn, moved by her appearance to stare at her, and forget the road. At such times her reaction was the opposite of that which anyone could expect. She would say nothing, and stare back at me, face tinged with a smile, until I, coming back into my mind, would realize: I am driving off the road: we are at our deaths! At this very moment I am inches from the edge of the road! Then, I would swerve, and save us, and we would continue. This must have happened nine or ten times, and she never spoke a word about it. She would watch me as I drove and we would talk of other things. At first when we were traveling quickly, it was difficult to hear one another, but when we had gone beyond the city some ways, the roads were all narrow and curved, and then we drove slowly for the most part. When she didn't sit beside me, there were other places she would sit, and in each she appeared to my eyes quite remarkable. In a sense, I am sure, it is true that she was not beautiful at all, not, as someone would say, a beautiful girl. Rather, she was the utmost extension of an idea of what a particular sort of girl should be. For me, it happened that this was the very type for which I had no defense, none at all. She would climb over the seat and sit amongst the suitcases in the backseat, sprawled out almost flat. Then she would look up into the sky and sigh, and speak to herself. I could hear almost nothing that she said then. At those times, I adjusted the mirror, so that I could look up from the road now and then and see her. Likewise, in the

mirror, she could see my eye, so I told the interlocutor.
I said, the car was a bit of an antique. I explained this
antique car to him, there in the office, using my hands
to show its dimensions. It had broad bench seats—really
the most comfortable possible car for a drive like that.
Her family had the most perfect taste. They didn't own
anything that wasn't simply great. They owned many
things, many, many things and all of them were great.
I, on the other hand, owned almost nothing, and the
things that I owned were, although carefully chosen, not
the finest in the land. In fact, it happened when we met,
when I met Rana, that I was embarrassed to bring her to
my home. We spoke of this when we were in the car. She
was driving and she had large sunglasses on. These were
almost the sort an old woman would wear who wanted
nothing to do with the sun or anyone beneath it. She said
they helped her see the road. She said, do you remember
when we first met, and you wouldn't let me come to your
house? For three weeks, I kept begging you, and you
would tell me, all right, come to my house, and then you
would give me an address, and I would go there, and
when I had gone there, it would be a different house—the
house of a friend of yours, or the zoo, or a tea shop, or a
glovemaker. A glovemaker. She laughed. I never told you
to go to a glovemaker's shop, I said. I don't even think
there is such a thing anymore. Oh, there is, she said. But,
I did let you come, I told her. I did, but it was only after . . .
at that point, I told the interlocutor, she interrupted me to
finish my sentence. She did that often, so I told the
interlocutor, because she had seen an old film as a girl in
which the two actors, who were deeply in love, had as the
badge of their love that they would finish each other's
sentences. And so, it was in her mind, she was adamant,
adamant about it—that she would finish my sentences,
and that I should finish hers, and that it would be a good
proof. She said, it was only after your house had been
robbed. I didn't get to see it with your things in it. Well,
you did, so I told the interlocutor, telling him what I told
her, you did go to the house. I said, my house was robbed,

all the things were taken out of it. I had planned to invite
her and show her my apartment, which was really only
one small room in a boardinghouse, but I was going to
show it to her, so I told the interlocutor. I lived in a
boardinghouse, and there was only a feeble old lock on the
door—a double-cut skeleton key would open it, a key such
as you could buy—you could actually buy it at a locksmith.
You didn't even need to break in. You could go to a
locksmith, buy the key using the change in your pocket,
and then be able to open my door with no fuss at all. In
fact, I continued, I often suspected that anyone in the
entire house, in the boardinghouse at large, could open
anyone else's door. I was of the opinion that all the locks
were the same. I did not, however, ever, at any time, try
any of the other locks. I wanted to, but was afraid I would
be found out, as most of the other boarders rarely left
their rooms. They were mostly shut-ins. In any case, I
returned one day to find the door locked, but within the
room there was nothing at all. It was as if the room had
been cleaned out. My assumption was: There has been a
mistake. All my belongings have been thrown out in the
street. It is because there was a belief that I did not pay my
rent—and this must have been the opinion of the landlord,
and it was an opinion that he acted on. However, this line
of thinking gave me comfort because I had paid my rent. I
would be due some remuneration if my things had gone.
It would not be so bad, so I told the interlocutor, relating
my turn of thought. Yet, at the front desk, I was informed
that my rent was paid in full, that this payment was
understood, and that I had not been evicted. The manager, a yellowed, rancid sort of man, the type who seldom
clips his nails, who believes they need be clipped less
often than you and I do, he said, it has been happening
almost every day lately. Someone comes down here
complaining of being evicted. Really, it is just that a thief
has taken your things. You won't get them back, I wager.
I'd guess you'd be lucky to see any of them again. A
feeling that I had had before—a sentiment that maybe the
other people in the boardinghouse were shut-ins simply in

order to keep their rooms safe, now came again. I had
once inquired about putting a second lock on the door, but
had been derided. What do you have that is worth the
price of a lock, the landlord had said. So, I shouldn't have
invited her, I told the interlocutor. I had invited her, but I
shouldn't have. In the first place, to bring her to a shabby
boardinghouse—this was a joke of an idea. Who would
bring a girl like that there? But, once you took into
account that I had put a great deal of care, an immaculate
care, I felt, into picking various small and good objects
and placing them here and there in this room . . . The
room was quite tiny, and so it was easy to furnish—it
hadn't taken very much skill, just care, and I had done it
to the best of my ability. I had put things here and there,
and made it rather nice. I was eager to show the place to
her. I was terrified that she would realize the yawning
divide that separated her grace from the constant forced
bowing and scraping of my sad situation, which is to
every month, at the end of the month, in the last days of
the month, have actually zero money, and be waiting in a
fast for the time when there will be even a few coins to
buy anything at all. However, she had been so kind and so
gentle, that I felt there was something in me to praise, and
that furthermore, by showing her the room, I would show
her some hidden resources that I had—something about
me maybe she hadn't yet seen. Whether this was a
fabrication remained to be seen. In my life I had often had
such delusions of grandeur, and when the time came,
they were always knocked down. But, perhaps this once,
I thought, and then the day came when I returned to my
room, unlocked it, and stepped inside and found nothing
there. I had actually told her that morning, come to this
address at eight in the evening. It is a boardinghouse. My
room is no. 37. She was to be away all day, and then would
come straight here. The idea was that I would go and buy
two items that were good enough for her. One was a loaf
of bread from the best bakery in the city. The other was a
small piece of cheese from a grocer near the museums.
Neither one of these items would be at a disadvantage

anywhere. Even if they were to appear in my room, that low place, they would maintain the real integrity of their quality. I felt I could give her a good morsel of food and not be embarrassed. However, now there were no possessions at all. When I spoke to the manager, so I told the interlocutor, he said that he would give me a chair and a small table and a pallet, but only for the time being. He did so, and I was overwhelmed with the feeling that these were the table, chair, and pallet that had just been in my room. He saw my reaction and said, everyone here has pretty much the same furniture. Don't think too hard about it. Then he turned away. The situation was, therefore, that I was sitting in my room on the one chair, at the one table, looking over at the pallet that was pushed into the corner. A small metal device for heating things was in the corner. It was actually screwed into the wall, and they hadn't taken it. You remember, she said, as we drove in the car, it was the most beautiful thing I had ever seen. I told you, I said to you, she said, it was the most wonderful thing anyone has ever done for me. Do you remember my face when you showed me your room and your things? Do you recall how pleased I was? She was driving quickly, and I had to lean over the gear-shift to speak to her. I said, it was only that I wanted you to like me. Well, I like you, she said. What had I done to please her so? I asked the interlocutor. Well, I had gotten a sheet of paper, a roll, almost a spool of paper, a long spool, and a pen, and some tape. I bought the bread and the cheese and a small glass jar. I bought one orange and a very small strainer. I went back to the house. I laid out three or four lengths of paper, tearing each off, and put the food items on it on the table. I put the table by the window, where the streetlight would shine on it. Then, I went around the room and where each thing had been—where each of my belongings had previously stayed—I wrote the name of it on a small piece of paper, and described it, and taped a placeholder there. So, she said, when I came into the room, I could see what your life had been like. I could run about at my own pace and read your tiny handwriting and learn how the room had been. Then, you squeezed the orange for me to drink, it was sour, and you said you had gotten a sour one on purpose, that it was a special savory orange, and we ate the bread and cheese and lay in the dark. The road ahead dimmed to a tunnel and we shot through the side of a hill, and out again and we were high above a terrain of low hills on a mountainside. What had been a hill on the far side was now a mountain, here where the ground fell away. The road ran in loops to the bottom. In the distance, there, she said, is an inn. Do you see it? I could not. It is there, over that way, she insisted. I think we could stay there tonight.

―――――――――――――――――――――――――――――

―――――――――――――――――――――――――――――

―――――――――――――――――――――――――――――

―――――――――――――――――――――――――――――

―――――――――――――――――――――――――――――

The interlocutor coughed. I looked up over at him. You know, he said, we think of memory as a redeeming thing. We build monuments that appear to be monuments to this person or that person or this struggle or that, but really, do you know what they are? They are monuments to memory itself, so said the interlocutor. We want it to be meaningful that things be remembered. Everything proceeds from that. If we do not remember what has happened before, then we are powerless to give meaning to what is, day to day. Because, he cleared his throat, because we are all like the Vikings, hoping to be feasted for eternity in a mead hall, there to have our deeds shouted out again and again for the regaling of some fierce and terrible company. In fact, he continued, memory is not the heart of the endeavor. That is the human secret. Forgetting is the precious balm that helps us to travel on, past the depredations of memory. His voice slowed as he said

these last words. He drew a long breath. There was a bulb
overhead in a loose casing. Suddenly, it was very bright,
for the lights in the hall had been turned down. A man
stuck his head in the door. The interlocutor assured him
it was all right. We were just finishing our business.
Though we would be some time, it was all right for the
janitor to leave for the night. I will lock up when I go, so
said the interlocutor. The door shut. What is the rest of it?
he asked, and again I was struck by the horror, as I had
been, again and again, during my tale, that I was confid-
ing all this in my grandfather. It was inconceivable to me
that I would say such things to a man I had hated, and,
already distraught to begin with, I recoiled at the sudden
fear. Then, his eyes met mine, and they were full of sympathy. It was like that—when he was looking elsewhere, I
felt that he was very much like my grandfather, and when
he met my eyes, I knew him as this new person, a sort
of confessor. Do you need some water? he asked. He was
holding a cup. He had filled a cup with water and it was
extended to me. I drank it. We arrived, I said, at the inn
for the night. She was still driving. This was a territory
she had often passed over. She whirled into the parking
lot and stopped the car just about anywhere. She pulled
up and hopped out, leaving the car, as if it were a horse,
any which way in front of the inn. This was something
I liked. No one else would be coming, clearly. There was
no reason not to do it just the way she had. The people
inside the inn did not know us, but were efficient, kind,
effective, gave us the keys to a room, showed us the room,
brought us some supper, a dish of cold meats that was
more than we needed, and dismissed themselves for the
night. Rana said, Clement, she said it from the bathroom,
Clement, come here. There was a large bathtub—larger
than usual, one could actually stretch at one's length. This
was the sort of inn it was—a way station, for people to get
back the energy they needed in order to travel on. It must
have been there forever, I said to Rana. It has been for my
entire life, or at least as long as I can remember things, I
can remember it. She was precise in this way—and hated

to say things that were not true. Sometimes, she would
correct herself, days after having said something, it would
occur to her that she had not been *specific enough.* Then,
she would demonstrate the thing she meant, at length,
from several angles, to her satisfaction. I, who had never
been specific, for whom specificity was a dream, and on
whom specificity was wasted, was now the chief recipient
of her wonderful specificity. We sat in the bath, and
I remember, so I told the interlocutor, that she wanted me
to tell her about my hopes for my life. Tell me, she asked,
as she sometimes did, what do you plan for yourself? I
hated these questions, but I was always calm and quiet.
I always avoided them carefully. I had a plan, I said, once,
to be a ferryman. That lasted a while, then I wanted to be
a traveler, some kind of marco polo. What do you hope
for? I asked her. She said, now that we are grown so close,
I have begun to include you in my hopes. What if we were
to move to another city, one we hadn't ever been in, and
learn it together—we could learn the whole city together.
We could learn a new language, just to live there, and we
could speak that language together. We could start some
business, a business that we know, because it is common here, but the sort of thing that isn't to be found at
all in that city. Then, we could sit in the shop and now
and then sell something, and we would have a fine life.
I have enough, she said, to support us doing something
like that. We wouldn't even need to make money with the
shop. It would be our pastime. Then, every so often some
of our friends would travel and visit us and we could see
them, and at their arrival we would be so pleased. Hello,
hello, we'd say, and after they had been with us a time in
that new place, they would go, and we would be equally
pleased to see them leave. That's how it would be, she
must have thought to herself, before saying it out loud
to me—we can have a fine life like that. I am prepared, I
said, to go anywhere. I only want to know ten minutes in
advance. Why is that, she asked. Ten minutes? If you will
go, you'll go. You don't need ten minutes. Ten minutes?
She pretended to be wounded at the thought, so I told the

interlocutor. Only that I might bury a few things, I said. When I live in a place, I always like to bury some of my belongings in the ground near where I lived. Then, when I come back, I can have the sense that—if I like, I can dig them up. I don't believe I ever would, but it is nice to feel, even if everything else changed, one's few things are waiting there beneath the earth. Like bones, she said. If you were really brave, you might leave a finger or two, or an ankle. I would do it, I said, if I thought there was something there worth remembering that badly.

When we slept that night, so I told the interlocutor, I woke and found that she was gone. The bed was empty, and the room was utterly quiet. I had the sensation, such as one sometimes has, that I had been alone for a long time. I went outside and she was sitting on the steps, staring out at nothing. It was dark—country darkness, near complete darkness, and she was sitting in it, by herself. Rana, I called, Rana. I am here, she said, and she was there by my feet. I had walked clear to the end of the porch, and she was there. I sat, and reached out, Rana, and found her. I can't see you at all. I can't see anything, she said. Her voice was hoarse, and when I pressed against her I could feel that her face was wet. Are you all right? It is nothing, she said. I was thinking of my parents. But, if we go to a foreign city, I said, it would be a long time before you saw them again. But, I would, she said, in that situation, I would see them again. What do you mean? I asked. Nothing, she said. Let's find our way inside. Then, we were driving in the car, I was at the wheel, the sun was overhead. I had on a burlap sack of a shirt that fluttered all around me. She wore a light gray dress that was sewn to her—it didn't flap at all. We shot along the road beneath a frighteningly blue sky. The forest gets deeper, and deeper, I shouted. Deeper and deeper. We are almost there, she told me, as we stopped for gas. She filled the tank, and the two gas station attendants stood watching her, eyes glued to her, as she insouciantly pranced about the gas station,

filling the tank in the absolute most tom-boy fashion. My
father bought this place when he was still a child, with
his inheritance. This statement she repeated, as we pulled
up the drive, as I stopped the car in front of the lodge,
and as we got out. I carried the bags up the wide steps
and she repeated, my father bought this place when he
was still a boy. His father passed away, his mother, too,
and he no longer wanted to live in the house where he
lived. His aunt had come to take care of him, but he was
not to be taken care of. He would take care of himself, so
she said, I told the interlocutor. He sold the house that
he lived in, and bought this one, and moved himself and
his aunt there. It was an important place to him, and so
I spent most of the summers of my childhood here. The
truth is, I haven't been back in five or six years. It hasn't,
she said, even occurred to me to come here. But now, I am
finally here again. My father would have happily joined
us. She seemed caught up by the thought. How he would
like to be here again. You could contact them, I said, and
have them come down. Somehow the thought frightened
her. It would be . . . she said, hesitating, and then she fell
hesitating into a sort of not-speech about the matter. She
was turning it over in her mind and instead of telling me
what she had arrived at, she did the opposite. She walked
away and began to explore the house and see the state that
it was in.

I am not crying, she insisted. I had found her in an
upstairs bedroom, and she was curled on the bed, shaking. You are not crying, I said, but your face is wet. Her
face was wet, I told the interlocutor, and she had been
crying, but I didn't know why. I used my sleeve to wipe
her nose and mouth, and kissed her, and I did everything
I could to comfort her there. When we made love, I said
quietly, it was a brutal, brutal thing. It was never easy. It was
an intimacy so terrible that it left us both reeling. The first

time we did, in my room at the boardinghouse, we could
neither of us move for some hours. We lay there, entirely
spent. When I found her in the upstairs room, it was
almost the same. It was as though there were little walls
that would spring up, again and again, between us, and
the moment of our physical love was the actual breaking
down, the shattering of them. She frequently would cry,
abjectly weep, and it would be terror and grief that would
turn to joy or joy to grief. She said to me, once, afterward,
that she thought nothing physical should ever be easy. It
should all be difficult. It should all be done with the maximum effort, utterly helplessly. I said that I would do, as
always, exactly what she thought was right. She said, don't
do anything I say, ever. She turned her face away from
me. She was crying again and could not be comforted. We
rose after an hour or two and went and saw to the house.
It was a hunting lodge. I hadn't been in a hunting lodge,
didn't know there were hunting lodges, but it was one.
There were various trophies on walls, and guns in places.
There was a mudroom, and natural wood chairs and
rocking chairs on long porches that knelt to the ground.
The trees were fabulously old, older than practically any
trees I had seen in quite a long time, and the house had
apparently been built amongst them. The porch had a tree
halfway through it that supported the porch roof. See, she
said, here is what I wrote in the tree, and she showed me
her name there. Raina. I wrote it this way when I was,
when I was, it would have been, from nine to eleven. I
wanted some self-determination, so I changed my name.
Then, a dreadful thing happened. What? A girl came to
the school where I studied, and her name was Raina.
I didn't like her at all. She was extremely vulgar, but she
liked me, and she liked that we were alike. I remember
the teacher saying her name, saying it unnecessarily in
my presence, just so I would know that there was
another Raina about. I was horrified, disgusted. So, I
changed my name back. But, here it is. You should put
your name here, she said. She took a little knife from her
bag and I opened it and cut my name into the tree.

Clement, I wrote. See, I said, I didn't spell it differently, but I thought I might. You thought you would, she said, but when it came to it, you like your name. You couldn't write it differently. There is a sacredness to names. Sacredness, I said the word over. Sanctity, she said. I guess sanctity is the word, but it feels like the meaning is wrong. You are better now, I said. You aren't sad anymore, I told her. You appear fine, I said out loud to Rana, so I told the interlocutor. I don't know if I wanted her to be fine, or whether she was fine, but while we were there, I kept watching her to see if she was sad, and when she was sad, I would smile and divert her mind, and when she was happy, I would say, helplessly, I would say, oh, you are happy again. If anything, this reminded her of her sadness. I couldn't tell what it was, and she wouldn't say. There was a telephone there, but she wouldn't use it to call anyone. When I suggested it, she said, no, we have come here, and now I don't want to go anywhere, to be anywhere but here. This is the place for us. We have this house, and the little town nearby where we can buy our groceries. Tomorrow when we get up, we'll walk into the town. I feel weak now, but tomorrow, I think I will feel stronger. And when some hours had passed, she felt strong enough that we went up a ladder to the roof of the hunting lodge, where there was a sort of *viewing platform*. We can sleep up here, she told me. There is a thing that happens, if you are very still. The bats pass by overhead, just inches away. I went and brought up some sheets and a pillow. I found a pile of old coats, and I brought them up. We can sleep on these. This was my coat, she said. She held one up. Look, I can still fit in it.

The truth is, I said to the interlocutor, she was perfectly right. When she mentioned the possibility of bats, I did not entirely believe her. I thought she might be speaking metaphorically, or just exaggerating a childhood memory that would never need to bear any proof. However, when we lay there on our backs, looking straight up into the night sky, bats flew past. They flew past. A fabric of stars such as you have never seen, impossibly far, and yet spread before you so clearly, all from right to left and up and down. You felt it had been placed there, so particularly were all these distant objects put into relation to one another. And then—bats, just inches away, tearing past. She said that it would happen, and it did. The bats flew past—not one or two, but dozens and dozens. It went on for at least an hour, just at sunset. I can't believe it, she said to me, clutching at my arm and pushing against me. She pulled herself up until she was on top of me, and her nose pushed into my cheek. She said, all these years and it is just the same, the bats pass overhead. I imagine they come out of the same caves, they live in the same colonies. I imagine these bats are descended from the bats that I knew, the bats that passed just inches above my face on summer nights fifteen years ago. Once, she said, my brother and I set out one morning to go and find those caves. We told my father. We put on our coats and packed a rucksack, and set out, and there on the porch, where he was sitting, reading, we told him we were off to find the caves. He bid us goodbye and told us that if we found them, there would be a choice then. It is the choice that people have when they find the thing for which they are looking. Will you come back. Then, my father said, you should decide in our favor, in what I would call our favor, in favor of the continued life of our family, and come back. You should not stay there with the bats. I will definitely stay with the bats, my brother said, if we find them. In that case, said my father, I take back my blessing. I hope you wander lost for some hours, and then stumble back here in time for supper. Of course, Rana continued, that is what happened. We had an idea of waiting until dark and using a flashlight to judge the direction of the bats' flight, but we grew afraid as the night started to fall. When supper came, we were both to be found at the table. I assume, then, my father said, that you did not find the bats, as I hope that you are now, and will always be, a man of your word. This he told my brother, regarding my brother's proposed domiciling with the bats. You have to understand, Rana said, that all of this is very funny. To my family, it is very funny. It is also something we never would laugh about, or talk about, or even mention. I only tell it to you now so that you can get to know me better. I want you to know me. She threw herself onto me, biting and scrambling with a feigned indignation.

In the morning we woke early, as everyone does who sleeps outside, and she said that she felt strong. This was a thing that sometimes came, whether she felt strong or weak, and we would change our plans accordingly. In the city, I had seen her every day, but not all day, and I imagined, standing there beside her at the hunting lodge, that I had not had the whole picture. She had, in the city, as a way of course, saved her strength so that she was always *feeling strong* when she saw me. The other things that she said she had been doing in the day, perhaps she had not been doing all of them, or at the very least not with her whole strength, and with breaks. Now, though, in the morning, we stood there in the morning light looking off down the mountain, she had her strength, so she said, and we were to walk in the town. This I told the interlocutor. Where the town was, it was positioned nearby the hunting lodge. Her father, being a boy at the time, had romantically been drawn to places not in the town. His parents had both died in the town. He preferred, then, living with his aunt and guardian, to move to a place beyond the town. Yet, he wanted to be able to observe the town. He had lived there all his life. The town was what he knew. He wanted to be near it, and yet to be apart from it. He took up residence in the hunting lodge, and modified it, with his own plans and the help of architects. He built the porch out into the trees. He raised a platform on the roof. He extended the back to reach out over a stream, so that there is a room actually in the house through which a stream flows. Rana told me all this as we walked into the town, I explained. She loved her father dearly, I could tell. How did it happen, I asked, that his parents died. My grandparents, she said. Yes, your grandparents. Sitting there, speaking of grandparents with a man who looked like my own grandfather, I felt an odd resonance. Perhaps once, I would have said it out loud, actually confronted this person to whom I was speaking, explained it to him, but I was weary and I felt very old. That, I did say out loud. I said to the interlocutor, I feel old. It's the thing that is most often said to me, he replied. But it isn't you that is old. You aren't the thing that needs to change. It's that you are overcome by your situation, by the way the world has descended on you. There is much in you that is young and new—and not just in you. In any person, even the oldest conceivable person. That's what it means to be living—to engage with the cacophony of objects. The interlocutor handed me a cloth to wipe my face. Can you repeat, he said, the last portion. You were speaking very quietly and I couldn't hear you very well.

———————————————————

———————————————————

———————————————————

———————————————————

I don't want to talk about them, she said, bitterly. Holding the cloth that he had given me, I told the interlocutor this, the bitter thing she had said. Standing there on the wooded slope fast by the hunting lodge, I told her, I can wait. But, a moment passed and she said very cleanly, as if she had cleaned off the sentence with a brush and then handed it to me, *my grandfather went first, and she followed him after a week.* We went on, she held my hand, but didn't speak. We walked slowly, and it was mostly down one hill or another. In the town, Rana was recognized at every place we went. First, at the grocery store, by the clerk, a young man of about our age; he said, Rana. He said it in a very unadorned fashion. Rana. Outside the grocery store, she commented on it. Do you hear the local accent? I said, I think I do. You can tell, she remarked, that someone is from here, if it sounds like they are narrowed in on what they are saying—as if they are saying it after having thought about it for a long while. It isn't so much an accent, I started to say, as . . . a mannerism, she said. A collective mannerism, that's right. I used to play with that boy. I think he was in love with me. We went on into the next place where she was to be recognized. That was a store that sold sweaters and other things of wool. She bought a long wool sweater for me, worked all about the shoulders with patterning. Everyone who comes here, she said, must buy a sweater. The girl there, who was extremely pretty, told Rana that she shouldn't pay. Rana brought the sweater to the counter and tried to pay, and the girl would not accept her money. It became clear that they knew one another. Take it, this girl said. I thought to myself, she must be the most beautiful girl in the village, even as she said to Rana, Rana, I haven't seen you in so long. Then, they talked for a little while, and I went outside. I could see them giving me furtive glances, these two utterly elegant people. They must have been speaking about me. In my heart, then, a sort of hollow but steely pride that Rana would want to be seen with me. She came out and we continued on. There was a small store that sold wine and had some chairs and a few tables inside and outside. Here we are, said Rana. This is where my father would sit, when we came here in the summer, she said. He'd sit here and play backgammon all through the summer with other old men. There were no old men there at that moment, so I told the interlocutor, relating the situation in the village. The place was largely unoccupied. Let's sit, she said. So, we sat there, and the proprietor came out and brought us two glasses and a carafe of wine. It is very good, she said, without pouring or tasting it. This town has a reputation for wine through the whole world. If you like wine, you will enjoy it very much. You seem

happy, I said. You are doing all right. I feel good, she said.
I haven't been here in such a long time. It is a good place
to come to. It is nice that some things can't be taken away,
as long as . . . She poured the wine into the glasses and we
sat there. The proprietor came back over. I am sure of it,
he said, I am sure you are Rana Nousen, Andro Nousen's
daughter. I remember you. She accepted this, and she said
his name to him, and he was very pleased. He explained
that they don't come to his place to play backgammon
anymore, the ones that did, because they were mostly
dead. The younger people aren't interested, but we do all
right. We get enough custom in the evenings, he said to
us, so I told the interlocutor. We sat at a table on the side
of the main street of the little mountain town and heard
this man's estimation of his business, so I said. But, your
father, the man asked. He is still living? He is, said Rana.
Hers is, he said to me, a very delicate family. All the
aristocracy from these parts are. He gave her a familiar
nudge with his elbow. It is something you are quite used
to, I know. We have all become used to it. Your brother's
death, though, was too early. Much too early, he said. He
was here often. He would come with your father, nearly
every day, carrying that monocular, what was it—that
shooting glass that your father had given him. He was
always staring off through it. Much too early, much too
early. He coughed a short, harsh cough. Much too early.

You must be used to what, I asked. What brother, I asked.
I didn't know you really had a brother. What was he
talking about? The proprietor had gone away, and we sat
there in that village, at a table in the street, and Rana was
looking at me with her bright, lovely face, and her hair was
falling all over, and her posture in the chair was graceful,
so graceful, I almost couldn't bear it. I could see that she
was tired again, I could see she didn't want to speak, but
she was bearing up, and part of it was in her raising up

of her chin and her shoulders, and it stretched her dress against her body and she was breathing in and out with difficulty. If I had ever loved anybody, I thought to myself, and I kept saying, tell me. What did he mean? She shook her head. I wasn't hiding anything from you. I just didn't mention it yet. My brother, he died when he was a boy. I told you about him—with the bats, the bats. He died of the same thing as my grandparents. It goes that way in my family. Most of them die of the same thing. That's why he asked about my father. He is not very old, though, my father. He is not going to die. What is it, I asked. Now we were walking again. I was carrying a canvas bag with all the groceries, and a flask of the wine over my shoulder, and we were walking back up the hill to the lodge. We would stop occasionally so she could rest, and then we would continue. The exertion and the mountain air made her eyes bright and fierce, and she would look at me and it was as if the sudden sight of me pleased her. That was a thing that was different with her than with everyone else I had ever known. With everyone else, they would come into a room and I would be standing there, and they would see me and recognize that I was there, and then something would happen, an action or a conversation. It would proceed directly from their recognition of knowing me, or their recognition of not knowing me. Something about me would activate in their head, everyone I had ever known, and in the space of a moment, some action would occur and I would be enmeshed in it, or I would be separate, I would push myself away from it, and be distanced. That was the usual thing. But, with Rana, whenever it happened that she didn't know I was somewhere, or whenever she was away in her mind thinking, and forgot that I was there, then it would happen, so I told the interlocutor, her eye would come upon me, and an absolute leaping delight would rise in it. I would see that her whole being was gladdened. She had seen me—I was near! For me, this was hardly to be believed. I didn't know what it was at first, until I knew, and then it was a thing that I could only be grateful for—a thing I could never deserve. In the mountain air, she was sitting on a rock and she was looking at me, and her eyes flashed with that same light. It is a sickness, she said, that makes your body unable to defend itself. Slowly you die of something else. And because there is always something else, always *something else*. Stopping any one particular something-else doesn't call a halt to it. My grandfather died, and my grandmother, who was related to him—in my family cousins often married—must already have been battling it, and when he died, she gave in. My brother gave in when I was fifteen. Everyone *gives in*. That's how we talk about it, she said, my father to me, and my mother, my brother even, my cousins, my aunts. *He gave in. She gave in. After a time, it was too much, and he gave in. Then she had no choice but to give in also.* How do you know if it has begun? I asked. Have you ever had any sign of it yourself? She blinked and smiled. She actually laughed, so I told the interlocutor. Me, no. No, not me. I've always been just fine. Why would you think that? I said that she had been weak of late. She said, it is just the altitude. Haven't you felt weak as well? This was, she said, in any case, a good climate for the illness. That's why my grandparents had been here in the first place. The family had settled part of their estates here, hundreds of years back, because it was a good place for convalescence. Of course, she continued, all that land is long gone. Just the hunting lodge remains. You are fine, I asked. Are you? Stop it, she said, hitting me lightly on the arm. I'll beat you up the hill. Then, she went ahead of me up the slope, I told the interlocutor, and I could only hurry after her, burdened with all our purchases. When we reached the house, she was exhausted. Her face was sunken, and she could only lie in the downstairs daybed, breathing softly. I helped remove her clothing, and looked at her body there on the bed beneath me. I undressed and lay beside her. We are as far away, she said, as anyone can be from anything, here. Do you like that feeling? I asked her. I like it, she said. I have longed for it. I entered a state, so I told the interlocutor, wherein I was with her and I was

watching us both from a point beyond. Somehow, I could
see that we were in the house, going about the house,
making meals, eating meals, playing cards or chess,
sitting out late drinking wine and talking of nothing at
all, or sitting close together on a bench with our heads
inches apart, talking with great direction of particular and
very important things, these things I could see as from a
great distance, and from up close. I could see as though
out of my own eyes, and out of the eyes of another. I feel it
was some circumspection that had grown around me. She
said suddenly, after we had been there four days, I want
to make all of our plans. What plans, I asked. All of them,
she said, I want to make all of the plans that we will make
for our future, I want to make every one. I want to make
the plans for what we will do now, while we are young. I
want to make plans for what we will do partway through
our careers, when we are in our primes, and the world
has received our gifts with great gladness and even
approbation. I want to make plans for our old age, for
what we will do when we are old and the world opens
again—to the separate wishes we have then, when for us
everything will have changed, everything but that we will
still want—that I will still want you with me. This she
said to me, I told the interlocutor. This person who was so
far above me, not just in terms of wealth or birth, but in
actual human evaluation. I am sure of it, as sure of it as
I could be of anything, that if a group of the finest people
that had ever lived were to see to her and look her over,
speak to her and know her, they would set her high, high
above me, so high that I would never have met her or
known her. I said, I can scarcely believe that it did happen,
that we did meet, but we did, and for some reason she
recognized me as something like herself, although in this
I think that she was wrong. Where she was courageous
and strong, willful, passionate, clever, I was cowardly,
weak, forever bowing beneath the weight of things I did
not understand and could not. Perhaps I will be a doctor
in a small town, she said. We will find a small town where
so little is known of medicine that we can smatter

together some portion of knowledge and I could be a doctor and you could be my helper. We would do what we could for people, and not just for people. Perhaps it would be a place so basic that the same person deals with animals and people. Not a human hospital, not a veterinary hospital, just a hospital. She said this, laughing at herself in a way, laughing at her plans and her planning, but delighting in it. She had no intention of being a doctor. By this she was teaching me how to enjoy her planning, and her work of ideas. We shall take pleasure in everything, she was saying—in things, and in the hope of things.

Do you ever convince people to go through with it? After some point? I asked the interlocutor. He shook his head. Never, never. Then, he thought better of it, of this thing he had said, and he began to speak: There was a man who came to me, right at the beginning, said the interlocutor. I was not very good at this job, yet. I didn't know exactly how to go about doing it. No one did, really. We were still working out all those things, for ourselves and for each other. But, then, at that time, there were many people, as there always are, who needed our help. We could not fail to do the job because we didn't know how to do it. Then, at that time, not knowing how to do the job, we still had to do the job. It was in this way that we learned the work, and came to our present expertise. In any case, this man, this case that I am telling you about, he came to me first thing in the morning. We have a consensus, we who do this work, said the interlocutor, that the people who come first thing in the morning are the ones in the greatest

danger. It is easy to feel at night, or in the loathsome
stretch of the afternoon, that all things are near to their
end. But, in the morning, the bright morning, to wake
and go forth, and feel utterly confined to a brittle wash of
apathy or misery, that is something else. So, when he
arrived in the morning time, right when I was arriving, in
fact, I had a premonition. He was a librarian, and a poet.
He had published many books of his verse. This is what
the secretary said to me, coming into my office ahead of
him, in order to fill me in. I'm just filling you in on the
details, she said to me. Nowadays, I would never allow
such a thing. As you can see, we operate entirely without
secretaries. They are unimportant in this enterprise. Also
unimportant is—to be warned of anything. All that I need
to know, the person himself, he or she will tell me. And
that is crucial. The interlocutor became very animated.
He shook his fist. It is crucial that a person be allowed to
pierce the veil of their appearance and show me the
person that he or she really is, beyond the apparent state
of his/her being. But, at the time, he continued sadly,
I hadn't yet worked those things out, and so I was
forewarned. I called the man in. In fact, I had read a book
of his poems before. I actually owned one book of his
poems, given to me by a friend. They were wonderful
poems. I dislike poetry, as it is mostly bad, the interlocutor
confided to me, but when poems are good, they are better
than anything, better than cinema, novels, theater, song,
so said the interlocutor. He was speaking on and on, and
I realized I had lost track of what he was saying. I was
tired, and I had practically drifted off, but not into sleep.
I was just numb, sitting there numb. He was still talking,
and I tried to listen. He said, there are, though, only a few
good poems, and this man had written one or two of
them. I made the mistake of, during our speech, as he
told me what he expected for his life going forward and
how he wanted nothing to do with it, I made the mistake
of actually employing a turn of phrase that he himself
used in one of his poems. I don't know how it happened,
I must have, my mind must have been repeating the

poem quietly to itself as he spoke, comparing his speech with what I had read, and so the phrase was there, in the ether, and I snatched it up, trying to say something calm and gentle to him. But, rather than saying something calm and gentle to him, I triggered the worst conceivable reaction. Whereas before I had spoken, the place we were sitting was completely safe, was a calm, cool place for him to be, a sort of perch from which he could look out on other lives—a place from which he could go out without the clothing of his own life, to seek new things, whereas it had been that, as soon as I spoke, it suddenly became a place where he was known, where he might be remarked upon. In that moment he lost his humanity, and became a kind of organ grinder. It was as though I had asked him to dance like a bear. But, perhaps it was all for the best, continued the interlocutor, because, and the reason I am telling you all this is still to come, it forced me to come up with a formulation that could rise above the error I had made, and bring him back to peace. Just as you have a sense of yourself, and propagate that sense of yourself with your tales and personal legends, so he had the same. His was, though, completely poisoned. He was as weak as a child, not in that chair where you sit, but in another very much like it, not in this office, but another precisely like it, the mirror of it. I said to him, it is a fallacy to divide thing from thing, and it brings us all our pain. You have spent so long discriminating, finding the least possible, finest discriminations until you are capable of saying how this leaf differs from that, or the way in which a window, an unapproachable window high overhead, can contain all our feelings of helplessness, that you now seek only to divide, even when you think you seek nothing. We have a help that can be offered to you. You can resume, can easily resume, the business of being a person—not this person, or that person, but a person. And you can stay that way. We can provide you with an unspecific life. And so, for the first time, I broke the rules. We are never to attempt to convince anyone. That is not our job. But, I felt certain, sitting there, that I had taken away the purpose with

which he had arrived, and that he would never come
again. In fact, I convinced him to take the cure. I
administered it to him that very day. A digression, he said,
quite a digression, but an answer to your question. I will
always try to give you the truth if you ask me for it. He
adjusted his suit and looked up and down the pant leg, as
if there were something there. I had been listening to
him, but not carefully. I was still in the mountains, still
pretending in my own way to be sitting with Rana,
looking at her, and being looked at by her. So, I continued,
telling the interlocutor, saying to the interlocutor that
I have never had much thought for myself. I said,
continuing, I have always drifted from place to place,
thinking myself the least of the matters near to me. I have
never felt wronged when someone has gone on ahead of
me. But, she, she would feel wronged, I could imagine,
hearing her speak of me, on my behalf. What she thought
of me was far more than what I thought of myself. And
so, she wanted nothing more than to talk of plans. Her
idea of our future was a large and bountiful one. All the
ideas that she wove spread out like ink in water—we
would have a garden, a house with a garden. There would
be a garden on the roof of the house, and on the wall that
ran around the house. The paths would be made of stone
and moss. The house would have thick glass windows like
portholes. No, it would have no windows, none at all. We
would be living outside, essentially, in the garden. No, we
would live under the house in a kind of burrow, and
emerge now and then into a garden, a garden we spent
most of our time tending. It would be cool there in the
summer and warm in the winter. It could be outfitted
with fine wood like a nordic spa. It could be marvelous.
The windows could be paper. Whenever they tore, we
could simply place another window there. She became
gripped and her ideas ran on and on, on and on. I felt that
it was disturbing her, that this talk of our future was
making her weak. I was sure that she was growing
weaker. It seemed that the altitude and this flurry of
speeches, one speech after another that she was giving to

me or I to her, were tiring her. But, she became angry, and actually said coldly to me, if I didn't want to have such conversations, we need not do so. Of course, I wanted to—and so we did. Then, suddenly she was happy again. We sat on the daybed of the house, and she said, do you know what, I once earned a degree. A degree, I asked. A degree, she said. Sitting there on the daybed, she told me that she had once earned a degree in philosophy. The school where I went, they only taught philosophy. It was a college just for that. We would take courses in math and science and literature, but all of it, only in the service of philosophy. The idea was, she related to me, that everything is useless without philosophy, because, not having the proper philosophy, one will never know how to apply anything, how to apply the things one knows. Then, one can only mimic other people, follow after them. One can never apply anything in one's own right. She told me that she had taken a course with a professor, that he had offered a course on a man named Jens Lisl. Lisl was a great philosopher, she said, but he was mostly unknown, and no one wanted to take the class, no one but Rana, and so the professor, who already had a high opinion of her, he told her that they could make the course a thesis course, and that she could write a thesis on Lisl, if she was so interested in him. She laughed, telling me this. She had signed up for the course on a whim, because she liked the name, Jens Lisl. But the professor was sure that he had intimations of her seriousness. He called her to his office, actually to his office in the ivy-run school building, past the secretary, and all the other offices, and he sat her down and he said, Miss Nousen. I think that you are more serious than most, and I believe that you can make a contribution to the efforts that have so far gone forward in the study of Lisl. Lisl, Jens Lisl! She laughed. A name I did not even know. I had not read Lisl yet, I said. I am sure of it, he told me. This is a certain proposition. So, the last two years of my study, I did not take regular classes, as the way was with all the other students, but I took this one class, Lisl, with this one professor, and we wrote several papers, actually together, my contributions and his, about Lisl. I mentioned then to Rana, so I told the interlocutor, that I had never heard of Jens Lisl. No one has heard of him, she said. He is a sort of amalgam, as it turns out. He is an amalgam that serves as the core of a philosophy of inevitability. It is also sometimes called Modern Inevitability, or, the New Inevitability. It is a rethinking of determinism. We worked on these ideas for two years together. I was nineteen when we began, nearly twenty, and when we were through, I was twenty-two. I graduated, and never thought about any of it again, really. Sometimes, the professor sends me letters, but I don't read them. I believe, she said, that he was in love with me. You like to say that, I said. She blushed. She was always very serious. I do think that he was in love with me. I told her it wouldn't surprise me. Everyone would fall in love with her, given time. But, not if they know how I really am, she said, the way you do. At that point, I said, most would abandon you. I agreed with her, and told her that anyone, actually getting to know her, would get rid of her in an instant. This was extremely funny and we laughed for some time. I didn't tell you, she said suddenly, that I had earned a degree out of pride. I am not proud or ashamed of it. Like most things in my life, I am not proud of it, nor am I ashamed of it. It will just be hard for you to understand me, if you don't know that I spent a long time on work like that. When I am cutting a carrot you can think of it, and understand me better.

___

It was my idea the following day that if she was strong enough, we should take another walk into town. She wanted to, but felt that we should wait a day. I insisted that it would do her good, that waiting a day might just make her settle into a sort of lassitude from which she would only emerge when we had returned to the city, and then we would have lost the opportunity once more to see the town. We might never come back here again, I said. Oh, we shall come back many times, she disagreed. But, all the same, I forced her out the door, and we made it about a quarter of the way to the town before I realized what an awful idea it had been. She was absolutely overtaxed. She could barely stand. We stood there in a sort of alpine clearing, the path going up on one side and down on the other. Even the vegetation appeared taxed. I can go no further, she said. She didn't say anything. She would never say that she couldn't go on. It wasn't her way. Instead, she sat there and wept soundlessly. That was her way of giving up. I carried her back to the house and installed her again in the daybed. I got her water and some food. Then, I drove down into town to fetch more things, and returned, and made her supper. By the evening, she was feeling better again, although she was weaker than I had ever seen her. She had taken off her clothing. She wore just a loose pair of pants and a shawl. She lay on the bed, her head propped on a pillow. When I entered the room, she smiled. When I came again, with supper, she sat up and, leaving the shawl, came to me there in the middle of the room. She was mad with energy, then, I told the interlocutor. But, as soon as we were finished, she was exhausted again, and I had practically to feed her the supper spoon by spoon.

When supper was through, I told her about my visit to the town. I told her the wineseller had been talking to me about her brother's death again. She said that he always talks about it. He had a son who was best friends with my brother, and the family took it hard. In fact, the wineseller himself was probably her fifth or sixth cousin, related at some insurmountable distance. I had mentioned this thing, my conversation with the man, as a way of gaining territory. I wanted her to feel that I was conversant with the town and with the past. That even, separate from her, I could navigate the waters of her past and of her family's past, and that furthermore, to others I was identifiable as

someone connected to her. All of this was present when I
had said, the wineseller talked more to me of your brother.
But, if this statement had the effect that I wanted, I did
not see it. Rather, it plunged her into a sadness in which
she could think only of her family illness. She wanted to
speak of it with me. Now she would tell me about it. The
family illness. Before, she hadn't said anything of it to me,
but now perhaps it was good for me to know, and why not
from her, rather than from strangers like this wineseller,
who, after all, does not know the real account, or the real
ideas, but goes along filling in the narrative with his own
creations, or so she supposed. You wouldn't believe, I told
the interlocutor, how carefully she laid out these mental
objects, the mythology of her family's illness. She said to
me that she had never spoken about it to anyone before, to
anyone who had not had complete knowledge about it, and
so, she would be clumsy in talking. She was unused to
ignorance on this subject, as everyone in her family
possessed knowledge about it that predated her own. Still
she would try. She told me that her family was known, in
the places where they historically had owned land, as a
family of effete languishers. They were practically defined
by their illness. One after another, for seven hundred
years, as far back as the family goes, the illness has struck
again and again. The only way out of it, she confided, is
to die in some physical accident. Even in this age of
medicine, there has been no advancement. And why?
Because, she said, it is not worth it for the world at large to
put medical resources to work on a problem that affects
.000000014 percent of the population. I don't know if
that is the actual number, she said, but if it isn't that one,
it is one like it. During the Renaissance, the family had
been wealthy, much wealthier than they are now, and they
had employed doctors *specifically to find a cure*. Of course,
the state of medicine was such that it was useless. They
tried to cure it with alchemy. This was not a joke. Vast
wealth had been spent trying to save her family from an
illness using alchemy. If it had worked, her brother would
still be living. In fact, before that, before her brother's

death, when she allowed herself to think about the illness more often, it had occurred to her, and she had once actually said so to her father, that the money had been ill spent. Ill spent? Her father had not understood. His daughter, eight years old, was standing before him, telling him that their fifteenth-century predecessors had misspent funds. What could she mean, so I told the interlocutor, that's what she said to me, explaining her father's turn of mind concerning his young daughter's statement. I told him, she said, continuing, that if our ancestors had set aside the sum used to employ those doctors, quite a large sum, and set those monies at compound interest for all of the time until now, medicine would have changed, would have become useful, actually useful, as it is now, rather than useless, as it was then, and we would have the money to employ scientists and doctors to find a cure. Her father and mother had enjoyed this idea very much, and had often brought it out as evidence of their daughter's brilliant impudence, relating it at dinner parties. So often have they told it, so Rana said to me, sitting there in my arms on the daybed, that I tired of it and never wanted to hear the story. But I tell it to you now, as it makes sense to hear it. The other idea that was had, and this was a very good idea—it was had during the nineteenth century, by some woman of the family who went on to be an abbess, who actually left the family to be an abbess. All the same, she had an idea for the family, as a young woman, while still with the family. That idea was: we could benefit from marrying others, and not marrying with the group of ourselves. Breed it out of us, so she said. Although this suggestion was taken very seriously, it could not be effected. Why was that? I asked her. The reason is this: almost no one in my family can tolerate the presence or conversation of those not in my family. Although we are in some sense a populous family, although in each generation there are between seven and ten children, *every house a full house,* she said, still it is true that it remains the same blood. Cousins marry cousins marry cousins. Occasionally sister marries

brother. And why? Because we are all so sensitive. We
simply cannot bear to speak with or be with other people.
Therefore, a feeling grew up in the family, within the
family, one never spoken of, that the illness is simply *what
we deserve.* She told me this and I told the interlocutor,
saying it with the same emphasis she used, *what we
deserve.* That my father, for instance, she continued,
deserves to die based upon his parents' inability to tolerate
the company of regular people. That my brother deserved
to die based upon my father's inability to tolerate anyone
other than my mother. But, what about, I said, you and
I have met and we are together. If we were to have
children . . . I don't think I need to tell you, she said, what
the general feeling is in my family about you. It is
regrettable, but we shouldn't hide from it. She laid her
head against my neck. It isn't your fault, she said, but they
don't really want to see you around. They have, you see,
certain things that they want to talk about, and they only
want to talk about those things, and they only want to talk
about them in a particular way. You could imagine
yourself, perhaps, now, as we sit here talking, thinking of
a way that you could isolate, through careful study, what
are the exact things that my parents, and their brothers
and sisters, my great-aunts, my great-uncles, the whole
clan of them, settled at a long table or beneath an arbor at
a gathering, would want to talk about, what those things
are and what they are not. You imagine now that you
could isolate, she used the word again, these things, and
that having done so you could take part, meritoriously, in
such a conversation. But, in fact, it just isn't true. You
would begin to say something and immediately you would
go awry. You would miss a subtlety of phrasing, and a
feeling would spread through the crowd—disdain. It
wouldn't be your fault at all. Darling, I feel that you are
their equal, that you are equal to every last one of them,
even to them all gathered together. Wasn't I the one who
said, let us go to a foreign city? Didn't I say it just yesterday
or the day before? I did. Yet, you aren't good enough for
them, not in the way that you want. And when I am there,

with them, it is even hard for me, much as I champion you, to listen as you put your foot wrong again and again and again. Even when we speak of something like, the last time you came to visit the house, you see now what a thing it has been for me to have you visit, and still, I had you visit again and again and again, don't you see what that means, well, when you last came to visit—there was said, my father, he told us a story about his work. You remember, he said that he was conducting an examination of the Hruezfeldt dam, along with two of his brothers, who are all amateurs by the way, none of my family has ever professionally done anything, nonetheless they are brought in to consult often on matters of every sort by government, because of their extreme expertise. You recall that he said the problem of the dam was not a physical problem, but an economical problem. The government itself, in its maintenance of the dam, might as well be standing there at Hruezfeldt with its finger blocking the dam. That was the manner in which the Hruezfeldt dam problem was holding back the province at large from taking effective action in any number of spheres. Do you remember what you said then, in response? She remembered, I told the interlocutor, the entire conversation, a conversation I had utterly forgotten. I had to tell her that I did not remember. At that very moment I wanted to be for her a person who remembered everything and who therefore perhaps, beyond all possibility, possessed a chance of earning her father's respect. But even in that one minor incident of our conversation about a conversation, even there, away from her family, I was forced to capitulate and explain that I could not remember what had been said, so I told the interlocutor shamefully. He looked on, waiting for me to continue.

Could I have a glass of water again, I asked. He nodded, and went out into the hall to fetch it. When he had given

me water before, I hadn't noticed him leave, but perhaps
he had. He returned and stood there, handing me the
glass. I took it and drank. He sat. I was embarrassed, I
said. She had never disclosed any of this before, and now,
there in the mountains, I felt we were coming to the heart
of my unsuitability. So, I told the interlocutor, there in the
daybed, she said to me, in complete seriousness, she said,
about my father, in that conversation in our house, three
weeks ago, in which he mentioned out loud that darling of
his mind, the Hruezfeldt dam, a thing which, to my
knowledge he had never done—always before he had
called it *the dam* or *the backbone,* already he had been so
kind and solicitous in this conversation as to mention the
dam by name—and you told him, fiercely, that perhaps a
different source of power could be used to replace the
dam, you said it loosely, easily, a different source of power,
and then the province wouldn't need to rely on water, on
that form of power, which after all was only one of many
ways. After all, during your time in the civil corps, you
had worked on other forms of energy, so you said. Water
was not the final ends and means. You said it matter-of-
factly and without rancor, but the offense you gave was
enormous and sudden. I remember in particular the
callous way you threw in this colloquialism, *ends and
means.* The whole table was horrified. My father reeled
back in his chair. Make the Hruezfeldt dam, the
enormous Hruezfeldt dam, into a sort of architectural
folly? Declare the work of our hands, of our fathers'
hands, and of their fathers' hands, all some sort of
mistake? The Hruezfeldt dam? Was I speaking about that
dam or about some other? It had been frightening, said
Rana, to hear my father spoken to in this way, and indeed,
she had never seen him respond in that manner to
anyone, never having needed to. You recall that I spoke for
you, saying that, of course, we were speaking extremely
theoretically about it. We, in the dining room of a house
nowhere near Hruezfeldt, some of us never having even
been there, never having even seen the dam itself, were
extremely theoretically discussing it. I told him, she said,
that this young man, you, understood the matter was not

the Hruezfeldt dam, but the province itself and the
political map. Perhaps, I suggested, she told me, perhaps,
I said to my father, that an alternate suggestion was to
redraw the political map of the province. So she said to
me, remembering her interaction with her father, and so I
told the interlocutor. Do you recall, she said, how, as soon
as my voice, with its known cadence, rose in the family
dining room, my father appeared assuaged? Do you recall
how as the gentle good sense of my measure, so quickly
suggested, washed over him, he fell at peace at once. He
merely nodded, and took another bite of his food, the
matter forgotten. The only glimmer of it was when we
rose from the table and he dismissed himself, he went to
bed early. Do you remember it? She pressed my hand,
there on the daybed. It wasn't your fault, she said, but you
simply can't understand him, or any of them. It would be
like trying to run a race beneath a road while the rest of
them were running upon it. You would always finish last.
There we were, sitting in the lodge that her father had
bought as a child, and I had learned this truly momentous
thing: I would never become a part of her family. Also, I
learned a corollary and equally momentous thing: she did
not care. We would go away together and never see any of
them again. She would make occasional trips back to see
them, but I would not be in attendance. There would be
no reason for it, she said. She delighted in planning these
details of our life. For her, my absolute rootlessness, the
fact that I had no family, had little connection to anyone,
lived in a boardinghouse, wrote inconsequential ideas in
little notebooks, and generally was beneath all notice—for
her, that was wondrous. My very nonentity made it easy
for me to be assimilated instantly and totally into her
plans. She was one, I confided in the interlocutor, who
could not speak of something if there was the least chance
it was not realistic. She did not want to waste her time in
unrealizable projects. For her, she could take no joy in
them. All the same, with her family's vast wealth, many
projects that seemed to me from the get-go foolish or
impossible, were to her completely sensible, inevitable

even. That I could be without a doubt incorporated into her plans made it easy for her to chart with pleasure the things that she would want to do, and made it conceivable that these plans, fleshed out in her mind, could be said out loud to me, and related. I have never before, she told me, planned *with* anyone. Even my brother, whom I loved dearly, and even all my other brothers and sisters, who were already grown when I was a child, even they have never heard me plan. They believe that I have no plans, that I go from day to day planless. Of course, to them, this is sensible. They live extremely coherently within the traditions of our family. You will, I'm sure, meet them all briefly, at one or another family event where you are absolutely required. You will see that they are of a piece. I am to some degree viewed as a wild person. I have had friends, for instance, who are not in the family. This is a liberty my mother never had. Indeed, I went to school outside of the home, another strangeness. You could say that I was a sort of experiment that my father made. It has turned out well, I told her. Yes, very well, she agreed. Shall we go outside, I asked her, for it had begun to rain, and the raindrops were sounding on the porch roof. I helped her to a chair on the porch and we sat there, staring out into the rain. Sometimes, she told me, I feel that we are in the clouds here. Of course, it's nonsense. We are not that high up, but I sometimes enjoy thinking that we are. I looked out at the clouds, and I felt that she was right. She was right that we were in the clouds, and that we were not in the clouds. This occasioned a small happiness that ran along my spine and out to the cuffs of my shirt. Rana looked at me very seriously, then. That chair was the chair that Seamus Mendols always sat in. He was my father's rival. He would visit and they would argue, angrily, for hours. Nothing was good enough for him. He was angry at my father for not living up to what Seamus Mendols had expected for him. He was angry at my father for having children who had failed to do things as great as the things that my father ought to have done, the things my father had not done, but that Seamus Mendols had expected of him. Seamus Mendols could drink any amount of liquor and get nowhere near drunk. He could reason like a logician, and he picked apart everything that anyone said, as if it were a necessary function of the conversation, that it be reduced to its barest, most functional essentials. The lessons in logic that we all received, even my father, a so-called finished person, a true gentleman, the lessons we received from Seamus Mendols during the summer months of my childhood, were truly something. Seamus Mendols hated the days of the week. He disliked the base-ten numbering system. He argued against clothing that required zippers or snaps. He was writing a book, had been writing a book forever, the publishing of which, at some point in the future, would be a great corrective. No one but my father had seen this book. He would not speak of it, but sometimes Seamus would say to my father, in passing, as they spoke of something else, *as in 3:12:92*, referring to a passage. Then, my father would nod, and understand, so thoroughly had he read this work of Seamus Mendols. My brother was inadequate. To Seamus Mendols, my brother was a sort of joke. My sisters and brothers who were long grown, but whom Seamus Mendols had watched grow, sitting on that same porch, long before my birth, they were, if anything, richer jokes than my brother was. However rich the joke of my brother was to Seamus Mendols, the sisters and brothers who had preceded him were richer. That so many little beings could issue forth from my father, and none of them, not a one could make any motion to complete *the work that was my father's to do* was to Seamus Mendols a frightening, sad, and inevitable confirmation of the world's slothful indifference. Of the world's impassive, perfect indifference. Its slothful indifference. He could not decide. He would sit in the chair repeating first the one and then the other back and forth. My own arrival, Seamus Mendols greeted with animation. He thought of me as a sort of antidote to the general horror of my family. She is your better, he would tell my father again and again. Of course, it was not true.

My father knows everything I know, and then beyond
that, he knows other things the existence of which I have
not guessed at, and he moves through all of it with ease. I,
meanwhile, make my small attempts. Seamus Mendols
saw these attempts and rewarded me for them, for each
one, with a cheerfulness that was quite rousing. It was his
idea that I go to a college, that I be educated in public
school. He spoke to my father, and I was their little
experiment. When Seamus Mendols died, at the house he
kept just up that road over there, my father said, I will
never come back. He has not returned to this town since
that day. That is how dear Seamus Mendols was to him.
My mother, my father could bear. He can speak to her and
live with her day in day out. But, I believe the person
whose company he most enjoyed was Seamus Mendols.
The chair you are sitting in right now is the chair he
spent years of his life in. There is no such thing as feeling
the effects of that. Seamus Mendols does not linger in
that chair. But perhaps you can enjoy the view, and
feel the import of it. When I was here as a child, no one
but Seamus could ever sit in that chair. My father did
not make a rule of this, nor did he enforce it. It was
unspoken.

———————————————————————

———————————————————————

———————————————————————

It rained all that day and into the next. When the rain
passed away, I made another suggestion: that we take a
short drive. There is an old mill we could go to, I saw it
on the road, so I told her. I have never been there, she
said, though I lived here for such a long time. We passed
it often, and a feeling of mystery has long lain about it.
The idea that we should go there, I love it, she told me.
Let's take some things with us and have a picnic. As she
dressed, I began to tell her about an experience I had once
had. Years ago, I said, when I first joined the civil corps,

I traveled to many far places. In one of them, we were
working to build a bridge that would connect two small
towns. The idea was that these two small towns, each
one on the opposite side of a river, would, when the
bridge was built, become one single city. Although there
had long been antagonism between the two towns—
a history going back decades, perhaps even hundreds of
years, of rancor, still it was believed the bridge would solve
everything. We lived in tents along one side of the river.
This was a relatively new part of the republic. There were
still measures there in place that did not exist elsewhere,
that no longer exist anywhere. One was prison. There was
another worker, an older man, who shared my tent, along
with three or four other older men. One day, he found
that someone had been going through his things. He
found that some old photographs of his had been taken,
photographs of his wife and child. I did not understand
why it was important then. It was beyond me, but he was
enraged. There outside the tent, he confronted the other
men, including one who he thought, he was sure of it,
was the thief. We were using heavy steel cable to make
the bridge, and there were pieces of it, cut pieces, lying
around the camp. One was in his hand, and he struck
the thief with it. To me it seemed an inconsequential
blow. The cable was heavy, very heavy, and the blow was
slow. I watched his arm travel through the air slowly.
The thief did nothing to stop it. He seemed frozen. The
cable went to the space where his head was, and moved
the head out of the way, it moved the head to a place
adjacent from the place where it had previously been. The
one who had taken the photographs fell to the ground
and was completely dead. He probably stopped breathing
before his body reached the ground. So, I told Rana, as
she dressed for our outing. She loved stories of this kind,
and I could see by the way she drew her clothes on over
herself that this was a good time. Where, for another
audience, I might have stopped then, seeing that I
had horrified them, for her I continued, so I told the
interlocutor. I told her that, of course, the man was taken

away. He was imprisoned in a place not ten miles away.
There was a tribunal that decided on his fate, and he was
put away. I worked on that bridge for another year, and
every week or so, I would travel to the prison to visit him.
It was a mid-size place, with a high electrified fence
surrounding it. I would come, and there would be a group
of other people waiting to visit. We'd all stand in line
and, at some point, would go inside. While we stood in
line, we would talk with each other. I remember the first
time I went, I was standing with a woman my own age,
whose husband was incarcerated. She asked me whom I
was visiting, and I told her that it was a friend of mine, a
man I had often played cards with. I got carried away, and
began to speak romantically about his fate. I was there on
the line, a young man myself in a place far from where
I had grown up, full of my own life, and in describing the
condition and affairs of my friend to this young woman,
I went overboard. I said that he was unfairly sentenced,
that he had had his reasons for doing what he had done,
and that they were good reasons. I spoke very rationally
and explained all about why he didn't deserve to be in
the prison, in a way that admitted no doubt in my mind
that we were all of us, she and I, and the others in line,
a part of an injustice. I imagined that her husband was
wrongfully inside, or I came to imagine it in the course
of my speech. Although at the beginning of my foolish
little speech, I knew that my friend was guilty, and that
this woman, that her husband was probably guilty, too,
by the end, I had been carried away. I had tried with my
speech to establish camaraderie with her on the basis
of this injustice. She would have none of it. She turned
away, actually refused to look at me, and said, my
husband is in prison for raping a woman who lived in the
apartment below us. He has no right to have visitors, but
still I come, I don't know why. I stood there in the line,
actually trembling. Now, I told the interlocutor, when I
said this to Rana, she was not at all horrified, as everyone
else had been. Each person to whom I had told this story
had been moved to distaste, had looked at me in a sad new

light. That I should have such a story and feel compelled to say it out loud, it was horrible. If it were true, then it was awful. If it were an invention, it was almost worse. Which was worse, the invention or the truth—actually, it was hard to say. That was the usual reception of my story. But, Rana, just brightened up. She had finished dressing. She was settling a light jacket over her shoulders. She said to me, I would love to go and see that bridge. Can we?

And we set out driving for the mill, and in the distance ahead of us, we could see the storm receding. We are pursuing it, I said. Then she reminded me of the storm map that she had bought me, and we fell to speaking of my room in the boardinghouse again. Have you, I asked the interlocutor, has anyone ever done something for you so completely beyond all possibility of repayment that you just stand there agog, helpless in their presence? That is how it was for me. When I brought her to my room, there in the shabby boardinghouse, a place where half the windows were boarded up—rooms in which people still lived were boarded up, a boardinghouse because people stayed there, but also, because it was falling apart, it was held together by shabby boards—I brought her there, showed her my room and its absence of things, and she in all her good grace was pleased, delighted, fell even more in love with me, and went off. That it should have happened that way was amazing, but what happened next was this. I went to work at the antiques store where I had a position, and when I came back at night, expecting the same—some pieces of cheap paper, a pallet, a chair, what I found was this: I had given her a gift, I had presented my life to her as numerous notes on paper, taped in the absence of things, as shadows of a sort, in order that she could see whom it was that she had met, when she had met me. For a long time, I had hidden my things, my gathered physical life from her, but finally I had gone to present it to her, and I had failed, I had waited too long, my things were gone; yet, I had created this simulacrum,

and given that to her in its place. Knowing her capacity, I
knew that she could take my descriptions and hold them
all gently up together at once, and that she could feel what
the room had been like, and judge me. I wanted that
judgment and so I had given that gift to her. Then, she had
come back in the days following, she had come back, and,
she must have had some help. I don't know how she did it,
how she could have performed such an action, but, using
my meticulous descriptions, she searched through the
city for each and every one of the belongings named and
described on my sheets of paper. Using the descriptions,
she matched each to an object as like to it as possible.
She brought these objects together, and set them down,
each and every one, in the place I had said they should be,
and recompleted the room that had been stolen. Somehow,
she had stolen into the room, bypassing the lock, and
she had replaced every one of my things. A framed
photograph of a lunch counter, endlessly continuing its
perspective off into the bottom right, a hundred stools or
more, punctuated again and again and again by a neatly
dressed sodajerk with a white hat. A small painting of a
rat, in the Chinese style. An old fountain pen, half size,
with a notebook into the binding of which the pen fit,
and in the binding of which there was a small pot of ink
actually bottled and held fast. A large Spanish folding
knife, tied in a cloth and hanging from a nail. A pair
of glasses of extremely heavy prescription, useful as a
magnifying glass. An empty birdcage, with a bone flute
propped in it. A small crank phonograph, nonfunctioning,
and two cracked records. A suit of clothes, finely
embroidered, for a child, hung on the wall. A map of the
Maginot Line. A canvas bag on a peg full of broken ivory
piano keys. A Venetian rooster mask. An old-fashioned
bullhorn, hung by the window, half painted red, half
painted green, with the number 71 in white emblazoned
on the green side. I had worked in an antiques store for a
long time, and had built up a small collection, a fine but
small collection. Somehow she had scoured our city, and
perhaps sent out to others, who could say, and had found

something like to every thing I had once owned. To these she added one item: on the table, she left all the slips of paper in a tall glass jar, and on the jar she put a note: *love, let us replace every imagined thing with a real thing.* She did not even need to be there to see my happiness. She was at her parents' home. I went immediately there, and she disclaimed it. She smiled to herself and said, someone else must have done it. Do you have another lover?

The mill was largely broken down. We stopped by the road and crossed a field of thistle and weed to reach it. As I did, I paused at the threshold, but she plunged in. From room to collapsed room, she went, eager, possessed with the power of the adventure. I went after, looking for her in bedraggled and shattered chambers. Though in many places, an old mill like this would have become the site of drinking, of vandalism, it was here so far from anywhere that it was only what it had been—a mill that someone had walked away from, or died in, that time had settled upon with all its weight. The glass in the windows was old, and thicker at the bottom. The mill wheel had fallen off, and part of it could be seen slumped down into the water. We are the wreck of what we have been, and the place of our own future demise, I thought. Immediately, I heard her laughter through a space in the walls, and I felt—lightness. What a fool I was to think such sentiments. Here I was in a derelict mill and I had humanized the structure in the most paltry way. My mind was so limited, I thought. Where I, standing in the mill, felt only grief at my own impending death, a death that was half a century off, so distant it could not even be conceived, she, on the other hand, felt buoyed. Standing

in the mill, she felt the delight that a world could be,
and that in it, a mill could be, and that in order they
should fall this way—world, mill, and then her standing
in a mill, with myself a room distant. I went to where I
thought she had been, and it seemed I was mistaken. She
was not there but on the roof, actually overhead. She had
been watching me. I climbed up with her, and we sat on
the mill, and wherever we went within it, it broke more,
and we left it worse than when we had come. I said that to
her, and she said, it has had some friends, now, though,
or at the very least acquaintances. Without us, it would
simply have sat this evening watching the road. Then she
laughed again, it is almost a koan, *what is the use of an old
broken grist mill.* We were quiet for a while. I could see
she had suddenly been overwhelmed. She was dizzy, and
sat all the way to the ground, so I told the interlocutor. I
should say she fell, but it was slower than that. Are you all
right? We should go back, now, she told me. Suddenly, I
can hardly stand. It is night already. A moment ago, it was
plain day, and now, night. It isn't as dark as that, I said.
Come on. We went back across the field, and though she
had skipped to the mill in and out of the high grasses,
she now labored as though under a yoke. I lifted her into
the car and got in beside her. She regained some strength
there, spread out in the car where we had had so many
fine times. I once thought, she told me, that I would be
a diver. My aunt went on a world travel at age sixteen,
my mother's sister, and in Mexico, she leapt from a cliff
and died. She was in a group with others—nine other
sixteen-year-olds, all from my mother's town. They all
jumped; the guide jumped. It was deemed safe. Every one
of them survived but her. She was found in the water with
her neck broken. I was young when my father told me this
story, so Rana said. I had been looking at old pictures,
and I found one of her, there, actually on the cliff, in a
bathing suit. The photograph was taken moments before.
It was found in the camera of one of the other children.
It seemed to me from the picture that she would be a
wondrous diver. The other children were gangly or squat,

ill proportioned. She was a sort of swan, just perfect—the sweep of her at sixteen was marvelous. I felt, seeing this picture, that she possessed the utterness of this word, *diver*. Yet, my father said to me, so Rana told me, that in jumping off that cliff, she had ended her life. I wanted to be a diver, too. I told him that. I stood there, a child, looking at a picture of my father's sister-in-law, his own cousin, who had died, the sadness of which he had borne for decades, and in the moment of his relating to me the tragedy of her death, I said, I want to be a diver, too. That is how I was as a child. I want you to know that, Rana told me, so I said to the interlocutor. She sat there, stunningly beautiful, in this beat-up old car. We were parked there in the mountains, where a mill had been built by a river, where the river had mostly gone dry and the mill had broken down completely. This place where people had lived had become completely overgrown. She and I, this wonderful girl, Rana, and I, had adventured there, and taxed her, taxed her to her utmost, and now she, terribly, vengefully beautiful, sat with her knees to her chest in the car, telling me of her childhood idols, and her childhood impudence. I think, I told her, that you would have made a spectacular diver.

————————————————————————

————————————————————————

————————————————————————

————————————————————————

————————————————————————

————————————————————————

————————————————————————

————————————————————————

I woke up on the sixth day. The night before, we had
talked of whether we would go back soon, whether we
would make the travel. I had asked her about it, and she
had had little to say—only, as you like. I am not ready yet,
she might have said. When I am a little stronger, or
something like it. I had misgivings, I think. I believe,
I told the interlocutor, that as I fell asleep, I had misgivings
about staying there any longer. I had suddenly come to
believe that she was not affected by the altitude at all,
that she, as a mountain-person, would never have been
affected by it. Just as I was dropping off to sleep, I told
him, my thoughts led me to believe that she was not
affected by the altitude, but was instead very sick, that
she had been all along—the whole time I'd known her,
and that I somehow hadn't seen it. But, it is easy to think
that now—to believe I had thought that, when, in fact, it
is quite possible that I didn't think it at all, but rather, as
we so often are, *I was on the edge of thinking it,* and never
came wholly into the thought. However it was, however
it might have been, I woke that morning in a bed
overlooking the stream as it fell through a sort of gorge,
the bed that she had chosen for us to sleep in, and I
turned over and tugged at her. I spoke to her. This terrible

and inconceivable thing had suddenly come to be completely and unutterably true: I found upon waking, that she had died in the night, at some point in the night, and I had kept on sleeping, knowing nothing.

That it could have happened—this dreadful thing, that I could have kept on sleeping while she was dying, and not noticed, not woken up, I felt a momentary hope in it. It couldn't be true, and if it wasn't true, then maybe she was still alive. But she was not alive. I thought of the condition of our night's sleep and her passing. Maybe she had even tried to wake me. She must have. She who was so perceptive, it could be, it could have been that she had noticed her own death approaching and that she had tried to wake me to speak some final thing into my ear, and that I, instead of waking, instead of acceding to her very last wish, had kept on sleeping, dumbly, vacantly, sleeping on, so I told the interlocutor. He handed me another cloth, and when he did so, our hands touched and he pressed my arm with his other hand. She did not believe, I thought at the time, I told him, that she was going to die. But now, I believe, I said to the interlocutor, that she knew all along, and that she didn't tell me in order to give us the maximum possible time of happiness. If it could be that our last days were spent weeping and carrying on—they would simply have been a blur. They would have bled into one another. She was stronger than that, and her strength manifested in this way: she would not tell me, did not tell me, and we instead spent the time planning a life that we could never live. Where she was in the bed, curled against me, one leg actually wrapped around a leg of mine—it hurt my heart to feel and see it. It was clear that while dying she had clung to me, had pushed as close as physically possible. And all this while I slept, insensible. I lay there for hours, not moving, actually afraid to move at all, and I felt that I wished I could not move. But, eventually I rose. I straightened her out, and laid her hands across her body. I shut her eyes,

and pulled a blanket partway up over her legs. Then, I felt
strange about it, and pulled the blanket down. I looked
at her, there in her nightgown, and I cried and didn't
know what to do. So, I dressed her in some of her clothes,
what clothes I could fit over her, and then I went to the
telephone and called her parents. Although I did not want
to, I did it, I told the interlocutor. I called her parents,
and her mother answered the phone. She recognized
me, and the first thing she said, in a terrible voice, was,
where are you. I said, I need to tell you something, and
she said, you don't tell me anything. Where are you, that's
all. I told her where I was, and she hung up. That same
day, they must have driven for fourteen hours straight,
her parents arrived with others, and they took her away.
They took me back to the city, and actually dropped me
off at the outskirts. They did not want to take me into
the city. There was a feeling, I came to understand,
that I was to blame. No one said, she would have lived
longer, but I knew that they felt, every last one, that I did
not deserve to have her last week to myself. They had
never understood why she had taken up with me. They
understood it completely, why she had been able to be so
free with me—that my not knowing about her death was
the whole of it. But why it should have been me, it was
actually unfathomable. I was special merely because of
my ignorance. That was what she had seen in me, so they
thought. Her father said to me, get out of the car, please,
and pulled up at the curb. I got out, and the car sped away.
It had stopped for the briefest moment, and then it sped
away again. I was deep in my thoughts, in the backseat
of the car, and then I was watching as the car drove off. In
the car, as we drove in the car, I noticed that her parents
spoke with the mountain accent. It was apparent to me as
I heard them speaking, as it had not been apparent to me
at our previous meetings. We had been driving, all the
way back, straight, fourteen hours again, with her body in
the car, laid out in a coffin. The car had been turned into
a sort of impromptu hearse, so I told the interlocutor, and
I listened to them speak, and they said things pertaining

to her treatment. They grieved in a very plain way with
one another, there in the car, in my hearing. My presence
was a difficulty for them, and they overcame it by simply
believing that I was less than nothing. Always, one would
begin to say things, to make regrets about her treatment,
or the decisions that they had made in recent months, and
then the other one, whichever one had not spoken, would
cut in and say, enough of that. It is useless. And then
twenty minutes or an hour would pass, and the very one,
the same one who had said that it was useless to speak so,
would begin to say again, but I think we could have sent
her to this hospice, or perhaps that doctor could have done
more . . . and the first one would interrupt, saying, it is
useless. There is no use to speaking like that. And all the
while I felt that, although I was in the car, although she
was in the back of the car that I was traveling in and we
were riding along mountain roads back toward the city,
I still felt, surely and completely, that I was lying in the
bed in the house with her wrapped about me. I felt that
more than anything I wanted that immediate feeling
to overwhelm me: the sense that she was totally and
endlessly wrapped about me. And simultaneous to that,
I could see, as if from above, the room in which I had set
her, and the place where she lay, with her hands folded,
and her face looking up at the ceiling, straight up, through
the ceiling. I was standing on the side of the street, some
street I had never been on, at the outskirts of the city, and
I sat down. I didn't even go to the curb, I just sat in the
street. I was wearied, completely wearied.

When it became dark, I walked to my house, and I found
that a note had been left there. The mother had written
a note, and the note explained there was to be a funeral.
The funeral for Rana was set, and the note explained
that it was a very small funeral. There would be people
there, but what was meant by very small funeral was

that I was not to come. I was not welcome at the funeral,
I told the interlocutor. I gave myself up entirely to tears
there, before the interlocutor, and I wept outright. He was
totally silent, watching, and then he spoke. I don't know
how much time passed, or had passed, as we sat there,
all the while that we sat there. When did all of this take
place? he asked. And the funeral, when did the funeral
happen? It has been going on, I said, these hours while
we sat here. It is probably finished now. The interlocutor
inclined his head and said quietly, then she has had two
funerals, I think, and one of them has been here, in your
speaking. You have spoken long, and given her a funeral
of sorts, and I have also been in attendance. I have been
a witness there, a witness of a kind. I wiped at my face
with the cloth he had given me, and sat inertly in the
chair. He sat, waiting. I said, finally, I don't want to live
anymore. Then, he took from his desk a piece of paper,
encased in lines—a formal piece of paper. He handed me
a pen. I didn't read the paper. I found its outline on the
desk, and he pointed to where I should sign and I signed
it. I wrote, Clement Mayer, on the sheet, and he took the
sheet. He put the sheet into a metal box on the wall. Then
he took out of his desk a little brown case. He opened
it and removed a single yellow slip. The paper was very
finely grained. He handed it to me. He said, this is how
it will be. These will be sent where they need to go. They
do not now have your name. These are not the ones that
will be sent. The ones that will be sent will be exactly
like these, save that they will bear your name. The paper
will be of the same weight and color and grain. I held the
yellow slip and felt it between my fingers. He took another
box out of the desk and opened it. This drawer he had to
unlock with a key. He did so, using a key that was on a
cord around his wrist, like a watch. He took the box out
and set it beside the desk on a short table. He knelt by
the little table, on one knee, and all his motions became
sharply practiced. There was a little bottle, and a syringe.
There was a rubber cord. He manipulated them, set them
carefully by. He asked me to pull my sleeve up. I drew my

sleeve up. He paused. I will tell you something, he said. I
always say this last. I believe it is a comfort, and so I say
it last, said the interlocutor. He knelt, holding a needle in
his hand, and he said, a quote from the founder, Groebden,
*Everyone wants life—everyone wants as much life as they can
get, and as bright a life.* He is reported to have said that, the
great man himself. It is often misinterpreted. He was not
saying this was the case, that *everyone actually wants life,*
you yourself know that's not true, but rather that it should
be. If animals excel us, defeat us in one thing, it is this:
they all want their lives. Life is given to each one of them
separately, and they all want it. We do not. And why? Your
life has been made up of chambers, a series of chambers,
so the interlocutor said, his hand on my arm—and in
each chamber it is difficult to remember exactly what it
was like to be in the previous room. You can remember
that certain things happened when you were a child. But,
what it was like to be there, to be a child, it really is lost to
you. Our world is a difficult succession of losses, vaguely
remembered, vaguely enshrined. The Process of Villages
has improved upon it. I say this to you, the Process of
Villages is also a world. It is an improvement on the
world. It is a house, a series of houses, a system of many
series of houses. That which is essential about human
habitation and human nature has been boiled down to
its core, and repeated until the proportions are exact. In
these places, you will slowly get better. I promise you that.
There will be people there who will love you, and people
who will deceive you. There will be people who struggle
on your behalf, people you will never know. All of this has
been set in motion long ago. But, it is only now, at the very
last, that you go to join it. You can imagine it that way—
there are people whose entire purpose is to help you, just
you, and only now do you go to join them.

Come, now, incline your chair at this angle, please. I drew
my chair over. Your arm, now. He tied the rubber cord
around my bicep. He drew the liquid into the needle, and

set the needle against my arm. I waited to feel it, waited, but I didn't feel it go in. We're done, said the interlocutor. He unbound the rubber cord, and helped me to my feet. Two men, orderlies, came in the room. I was dizzy. He nodded to them, and they helped me along, one on each side. We went out into the hall, ponderously through the doorway. My feet were under me and it felt strange. I felt that I was standing on the sides of my feet. I could feel my weight in my ankles, but nowhere else. I had been sitting so long, and now I was standing, standing outside of the office. The corridor was long. It seemed to go on endlessly, and where it went, the end was invisible. It was completely dark at the end. Back the other way, where I had come from, was there light? Where the building entrance was, there must be light. I couldn't remember anymore which direction was which. The way we were going, I could make out nothing. The orderlies must know the way, I thought. They walked surely, surefootedly, one on each side, supporting me, their powerful hands gripping me, holding me up as we walked, on down the hallway, on and on, on and on, into the darkness.

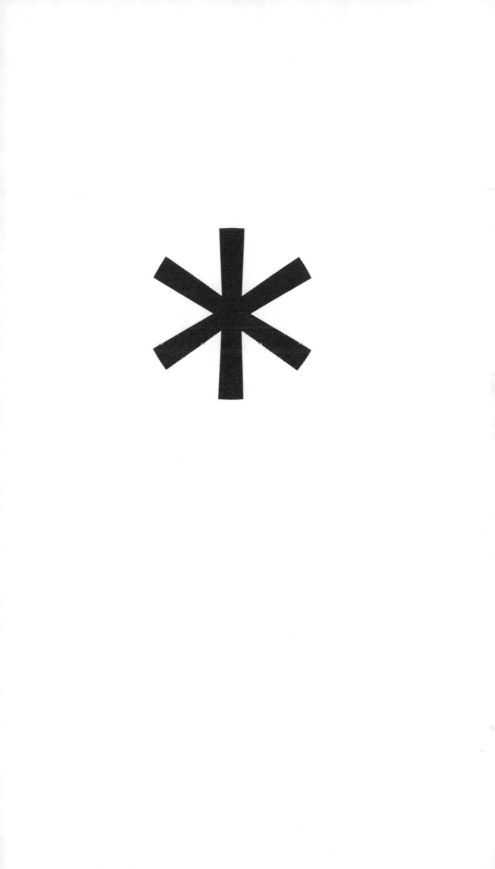

the

train

was

traveling

THE TRAIN WAS TRAVELING on a line of track stretched like black thread through the waste. It rattled and rode the line uneasily, its wheels crying out now and then as if goaded. The train was mostly empty.

Examiner 2387 looked in the windows of the compartments as she passed through the train cars one after another. One empty compartment after another. Almost no one here at all. But, her instructions had said . . .

She carried a neat leather bag, bright yellow, and her hair was wrapped in a scarf. Her hands were covered in thin gloves, the color of sand. Her shoes matched, and her stockings were a pale blue. She was like a blot of color set into monochrome film.

One compartment, another compartment, another. Another car, another compartment, another. A porter stood watching her. He looked her up and down, and smiled slightly. She did not smile, but looked him carefully in the face.

He pointed down the narrow passageway—further on. When she got to the door indicated she glanced back. He nodded. She peered through the glass. She rapped on the door and someone within called out.

THE WORDS TOOK SHAPE as the compartment door swung in:

What was it the older woman was saying? She said,

—Why, Hilda, Hilda. How nice to see you.

Or,

—Why, Hilda, I hope you are well.

The train rattled so, it is hard to say which it was.

The younger woman answered,

—Yes, Emma, yes. I,

Examiner 2387 sat down opposite the older examiner, whose number she did not recall.

—I, they told me you asked for me. I want to thank you for that.

—I will call you Hilda, said the examiner. You may call me Emma Moran, as you did. The names for this next town are different, but we will get to that.

They sat looking at one another, the younger patiently waiting for the older to continue, the older looking curiously at the younger as if to see who it was that sat there, right there, in the seat across from her.

—Hilda, she said. Do me a favor. Please give me the dialogue from outside the house, the night you left.

HILDA CLOSED HER EYES for a moment. She straightened her shoulders, turned her head slightly to one side.

—Martin! I look very different, don't I? I can see it in your eyes. You thought that the person you were going to meet was just like Hilda, the Hilda you knew. And then here there is this other person standing on the street looking at you. She snuck out of her house at night to come and see you and you don't know why. Now you don't even know who this person is, but you can't stop looking at her.

Hilda shook her head,

—No, no, that was the first time we met alone. Sorry, getting jumbled.

She thought for a second.

Emma watched her, smiling slightly.

—Okay, okay. Here goes.

—They took me away, they took me away, darling. Oh. I waited for you and waited for you, and you never came, and then I went back to the house, and Martin was there, and he was angry—he was so angry . . .

She shifted her voice.

—And then he said,

She spoke with a slightly deeper register, in a voice rather like the claimant's.

—Took you away? Who?

—Then, I said,

—I woke up in the back of some kind of closed truck. They were moving the bed that I was in. I was lying there, and we were stopped for some reason. I jumped out the back and hid, and the truck drove on without me.

—Then he asked me how I found my way back, and I said,

—There isn't anything out there. Just a road. It's just a road. I went the opposite direction the truck was going. As you approach the town, the waste turns slowly green. There are trees and grass, and then the town begins. I can show you. I don't know if there's time.

The older examiner laughed loudly and clapped.

—Just right, just right. Your performance in Case 42395D was indeed marvelous. It was perfect. I was very moved by it, and I can tell you that it was completely convincing. Do you know where I am coming from? I am returning from the board at which I presented the case. The fluency of your Hilda role was, well, as I said, marvelous. There were some there who interpreted this sudden excellence one way. They believe it is the flowering of a talent. You came to us, as you may remember, as a claimant, and one day, became an examiner-elect. Now, on the success of this role, you may continue on. I congratulate you. I did not tell the panel, however, what it is that I really think. Why? Because it is a thing that is for you, for your ears alone.

The train rattled and shook as they crossed pilings that supported the way over a series of small streams. They were entering a sort of marshland. Nothing but quiet in the compartment, and beyond the window, the train's heaving bustle, and the noise of insects and wind. A bird cried out from the twisted bracken, and its call pierced Hilda. She moved in her seat.

—Emma, what do you mean?

The older examiner spoke as if out of a long sleep.

—We were there together, I was with you, we two examiners, dealing with a man in dire difficulty. It seems to me possible

that you acted, that you were an actress, in this case, that the
man called then Martin Rueger, was nothing to you. It is
possible, of course it is. In fact, just that, that alone was your job.
But it is not what I believe.

She ran her finger along the wooden molding of the window.

—Some people forget, do you know—they forget what it is like
to be young, to feel things ruthlessly, terribly. If you forget that
much of life, well, I don't know.

She turned toward the younger woman and took her hand.
She seemed to be weighing something. A minute passed, then
another. The noise of someone in the passage coming closer,
then going away, past, away.

—What is it you think?

—I believe, Hilda, you fell into the role so thoroughly because
indeed you did love him. I believe that you really wanted to
help him escape, despite your position, despite your role as an
examiner in his case, despite all. There is something in you,
Hilda, that wants to rise up and ruin the world. You are the
sort, I think, who, when pouring water into a glass, will let the
pitcher overflow the glass, will pour it all out onto the table, if no
one has the sense to say, enough, enough, Hilda. If no one says
anything, a person like you will just pour the pitcher out. This is
my feeling.

They sat quietly a moment.

—I do not mean it as a criticism, she continued. Not at all.
Indeed, in some aspects, I also am this way. Yet, it does, if true,
present us with an interesting situation. It is for this reason
that I asked for you, that I called you back to this case, the case
of Martin Rueger. I have just moved him to another town. He
has a new identity, that of Henry Caul. He is settling, finally.
Soon, he will finally be settled. I wonder, examiner 2387
who masquerades so well as a Hilda, I wonder—do you want to
join him?

The young woman raised an eyebrow.

The examiner coughed.

—I suppose it is in some way disingenuous of me to ask in that way. Of course, you have been given the task. You have your orders. You're on this train heading to the village. You will do it. But, there are two ways in which it might be done. That is the essence of the offer I make to you. Two ways.

—I can tell you about it. I can tell you what it was like for me, and,

—Please don't speak, said the old woman. I will know it all by your choice. Be patient. The world isn't the place we are told to live in. It is another place entirely. We have both more choice, and less, than we are supposed to have. I will tell you a story about a play I once saw. Perhaps it will make things clear.

THE PLAY I ONCE SAW; OR, THE ONION KNIFE

Once, I saw a play in a city that no longer stands. This was the city of my birth. It was entirely demolished in the war. Every last brick of every last building was actually made to vanish by a single bomb. There is a sort of crater there now. I'm not joking. There is a kind of viewing platform, a boardwalk of sorts. You take the train to a little hotel town—a set of hotels that are perched where the boardwalk begins. Then, you go off down this wooden pier, out over the crater. The boardwalk extends all the way to the very center. It is far—maybe six or seven hours' walk, so most people ride bicycles. At the very center there is a little shop that serves drinks and sandwiches. You can sit and look down into the crater. There isn't anything to be seen there at all of what was. The city itself is clearly gone. In fact, when I went, I had a feeling similar to when I saw the Grand Canyon. I thought, my, how the world can be. This destruction was so bloodless it has come to feel like one of the great works of man. Of course, thirteen million people died beneath that bomb.

In any case, I lived in that city, and on one of the old streets that ran down by the courthouse, there was a theater, the Chamber Pot. I used to go there to see plays. I was a young woman, quite your age, actually, and I enjoyed seeing plays. I felt that there was in them the power to change the world. In such a mood, I went with a young man to see *The Onion Knife,* a new play.

The theater was very small. There were three rows of seats— maybe twenty could sit there. Then there was a small stage, about the size of a parlor. The actors took the money through the front door of the theater—there was an aperture, and gave you pieces of paper with a word on it. Each word matched a word on a sheet they had inside—and could be used once, so you couldn't cheat and just write the word on other sheets to get more people in. Also, you wouldn't want to. It cost almost nothing.

We had brought some cognac with us in a little metal flask and we got seats on the end of the first row. I had a fur coat then, and I was very proud of it. Often, I wouldn't take it off. I would wear it under inconceivable conditions, just in order to be seen. I had gotten the coat at a very low price in a store because there was a hole in it where someone had been shot. Apparently this thrift store would get clothing from the police ministry— evidence clothing that was no longer necessary. Yes, someone had been shot in my fur coat, but I wore it anyway. That's the sort of girl I was.

*The lights dim. A man comes out in front of the screen that
protects the stage from view. He is wearing a shirt and vest and
wool trousers. He holds up a card that says, Cecil. Then he very
deliberately moves the screen out of the way, revealing a small
kitchen and a kitchen table. At the kitchen table sits a young
woman. She is holding a sign that says, Lily. A buzzer goes off
and both signs drop to the floor.*

CECIL
When your husband returns, I swear I will . . .

LILY
He is not going to return.

She holds up a letter.

He says he has found a new life in Perugina. He will stay there
forever.

*Lily and Cecil dance happily all around the room. Someone plays
the fiddle offstage.*

CECIL
Then I shall make you my wife, and we will live happily forever.

LILY
But . . .

CECIL
But, what.

LILY
But, there is still the matter of the onion knife.

The two part and stand some feet away from one another.

CECIL
Oh, the damned onion knife. The onion knife. Why do you
have to harp on it? Haven't I given you enough things? Haven't

I done enough for you? And all it is with you is—the onion knife, the onion knife. You're like a drooling madperson in an asylum, sitting by a freezing windowpane on a March morning, pressing the side of your face to the glass and muttering, onion knife, onion knife, onion knife.

LILY

You lost the onion knife. I told you, never touch the onion knife and then you went and lost it.

CECIL

I brought it to work with me. You gave me a lunch that day: a little piece of cheese, an old piece of bread, and a very small onion. I noticed that there was an onion in my lunch. I brought the onion knife with me.

LILY

And you did not bring it back.

LIGHTS

A Third Person Who Has Not Been Seen, Appears On Stage
With A Piece of Paper That Says:

IT IS THE NEXT DAY

Lily comes in the front entrance of the theater. She makes
her way over to the screen that again hides the set. She takes
out a piece of paper and hammers it into the screen with a long
nail. She goes further down and does it again and again. The
paper cannot be read by the audience. She goes behind the
screen.

Five minutes pass.

The front entrance of the theater opens. Cecil enters. He goes
onto the stage and walks along the screen, stops. He peers at the
paper in horror. He tears it down. He runs along tearing all the
papers down. He turns to the audience. Tears are on his face. He
composes himself and carefully removes the screen to reveal the
kitchen again. Lily is sitting at the kitchen table, happily reading.

CECIL
Lily? Are you out of your mind?

Cecil runs to her, waving the paper.

LILY
No more than you.

CECIL
(almost weeping, reads from the paper)

Lily Caldwin has lost her onion knife. It has a serif G inset in
the handle. It is worn but extremely sharp. Please return it to
3 Welton Rd. for a reward. That reward is: Lily Caldwin will lie
down with you.

LILY
I think the onion knife will reappear pretty soon, don't you?

CECIL
Lily? How could you? You won't do it, will you?

LILY
Find the knife.

CECIL
I love you, Lily. You can't do this. I lost the knife, but it shouldn't be such a . . .

LILY
Find it.

*A Third Person Who Has Not Been Seen, Appears On Stage
With A Piece of Paper That Says:*

*IT IS THE NEXT DAY; CECIL DID NOT WANT TO GO OFF
TO WORK BUT HAD TO; LILY IS THERE ALONE*

*A knock on the front door of the theater, another knock, another
knock.*

LILY

(from behind the screen)

Can someone get the door?

*An audience member rises and gets the door. At the door is
an older man, perhaps fifty, slightly fat. He enters, somewhat
apologetically, looking at the crowd. He clearly sees the crowd,
and bows to them. He is carrying an onion knife, which he holds
up as if in explanation. He goes up on stage and knocks at the
screen.*

LILY

Come in.

*The man moves the screen aside to reveal the set of the kitchen.
The kitchen table has been pushed to one side, and there is a
mattress laid out on the floor. The audience sits immediately
before the stage, so the mattress is immediately before their eyes.
Lily is lying on the mattress. She stands up.*

Do you have the onion knife?

*The man presents her with the onion knife. She leaps with glee.
She runs about, back and forth, happily. She throws her arms
around the man suddenly and then runs away again to put
the onion knife into a wooden block that hangs from one wall.
She admires it there.*

MAN
There was the matter of . . .

LILY
Oh, yes.

She comes around to the front of the stage and helps the man off with his coat, which she places on the table. She helps him off with his vest and with his shirt. He sits down on the mattress. She removes his left shoe and right shoe. She removes his socks and his pants. She puts all these things on the table and then she comes to the front of the stage.

LILY
(with great joy)

The onion knife!

She unbuttons her dress slowly and removes it, setting it down by her feet. She removes the plain white underwear she is wearing and sets that, too, by her feet. She is completely naked, and possessed with a feverish sort of happiness.

The onion knife!

She turns from the audience to the man, and lies down with him on the mattress, where she fulfills her promise. The audience stays to watch or leaves, as they may prefer. The play is concluded.

—I KNEW THE GIRL, said Emma. Of course, I spoke to her about it later. The older man was actually her lover—in real life. He was also the director. The girl was the playwright, and the actress both. The husband from the play was just an actor they had found. This act of lovemaking in public, it might seem shocking now, but it wasn't so much pornographic at that time as, well, it was revolutionary. It was a reclaiming of the body.

They sat in silence for a minute.

—I've always felt, said Emma, that people misunderstand consequence. Anything really can be the consequence of something else. That's our human gift. So, when someone loses a paring knife, well, who is to say what will happen?

Hilda laughed at that. Emma laughed, too. They laughed together.

—At the time, said Emma, I thought that it was funny, but I also thought it was serious. Now, I just think that it is funny. Well, enough for my story about consequence.

She sighed deeply.

—Now I am going to present you with a choice, my dear.

THE OLD WOMAN went out into the hall and when she came back, she was carrying a little leather box.

She sat down.

—Hilda, she said. There is much to say, and little time. Martin Rueger has been renamed. He is now called Henry. Henry Caul. He is a scholar; that is his identity. He lives in sector B73, the sector we are even now approaching. I regret to tell you that he has been fogged since you knew him. He has lost function. You have gone through our training, so you know what the task of marriage is. You know that an examiner of excellence, feigning a role, may participate in a life in this way, acting as a sort of custodian for one who is somewhat absent. You know that it has been arranged for you to come and see Henry, to meet him again, and all going well, for the two of you to cohabitate. You are to become Henry's permanent custodian, for I will soon be gone.

—Henry loved you. He really did. And I believe that you, well, I said what I believed already. For you, with your inclination, to be custodian to him: it is clear that you can perform this task, and well. But can you be happy? Before, when you knew him, you could be equals. You could speak, he could answer. Perhaps he was confused—but he was also lacking information. Now, well, as you will see, he is changed.

—It is one choice, a choice you can make, to arrive in this town now, as you are. Your name is Nancy. You are to act as though you do not remember being Hilda. You are to act as though you do not know that you ever met a Martin Rueger, and certainly, you will receive Henry Caul as an entirely new person—one whom you will demonstrate affection for. You will win him over, and you will become his custodian. The train is even now approaching the town. This is the life you will lead, and there is something false in it.

—However, I offer you another choice. If it is true that you did love him, that there was something there, then perhaps it remains. Perhaps you would like another chance, a new chance. This is my offer: if you agree, I will inject you.

The old woman opened the leather case, and there was a hypodermic needle inside, a needle and a small clear bottle.

—You will wake up and you will be just Nancy, not an examiner, not a Hilda, nothing but Nancy. I will bring you to the town and you will recover in a separate house. When you are ready you will be brought to our home. You will reunite with Henry, and the two of you will share a new life, unencumbered.

The young woman stared at the needle as if she had never seen such a thing before. She reached down and shut the box. Tears ran down her face.

—No, she said. I can't. I can't.

She put her head in her hands and wept.

The old examiner stood and went to the door, the box under her arm. She slid the door open and stepped out into the passage.

—Oh, wait, wait, come back, cried the young woman. Come back. I think I, I think . . .

Her eyes raced helplessly back and forth over the shabby train compartment in a dry and awful panic. She flinched away from, but then looked up at the old woman, who stood, paused in the doorway. The train was coming to a halt. They were arriving.

—I think, I . . .

The old woman loosened her features. She stood a bit straighter. She spoke in a voice unfamiliar.

—Hilda, she said, darling, you were very sick and you almost died.

Hilda sobbed.

—Hilda, look at me.

She took Hilda by the chin.

—You were on the edge of death and you were rescued. You were rescued.

The old woman shook her head and a sad laugh fell from her. The train came to a halt. They had been in the wastes where there was no one, but now, but now . . .

Outside the train, voices cried out, one to another. A village of voices, men, women, calling out as if in human speech.

But another voice closer, closer, was saying, *what do you choose. Hurry now, hurry now, what do you choose.*

ACKNOWLEDGMENTS

THANKS TO:

J. Jackson & all at Pantheon.
B. Sweren & all at Kuhn Projects.
Poyais Group.
Godshot, Bonanza Coffee Heroes & Schokogalerie.

A NOTE ABOUT THE AUTHOR

Jesse Ball is the author of four previous novels, including *Silence Once Begun* and *Samedi the Deafness,* and several works of verse, bestiaries, and sketchbooks. He received an NEA creative writing fellowship for 2014, and his prizes include the 2008 *Paris Review* Plimpton Prize; his verse has been included in the Best American Poetry series. He gives classes on lucid dreaming, walking, and lying at the School of the Art Institute of Chicago.